RANDOM WALK

RANDOM WALK

RACHEL LULICH

Cover design by Christopher Doll
Interior design by Kyle Shepherd

ISBN, paperback: 978-1-7342379-0-0
ISBN, ebook: 978-1-7342379-1-7

This book is a work of fiction. Any resemblance to actual events, places, or people, living or dead, is coincidental.

CHAPTER ONE

It was still dark as they were driven out to the spacecraft in the launch van. Victoria Abrams peered out the window at the launchpad, her heart fluttering at the sight of the rocket standing there, lit up in giant floodlights like a movie set. It was beautiful.

"Look at that," Captain Jacob Mendez said from the seat in front of her, unconsciously echoing her thoughts. He pressed his face to the window, absently smoothing his reddish-brown hair and staring in open-mouthed awe. It was one thing to see the rocket roll into place in the light of day, knowing they'd be on it the following morning. It was another to be approaching it for the final time, in the dramatic lighting of the Florida pre-dawn.

Colonel Derek Williams, their mission commander and pilot, smiled. "That's our ship." *Our ship*. And it was. Derek looked over his shoulder at Vicky, sitting behind Jacob on the passenger side of the van. He had to turn his shoulders a little to see her, the bulk of his orange Astronaut Crew Escape Suit hindering his movement at first. Vicky was staring out the window, oblivious to his gaze, and he turned back to the view. Incredible.

The rocket, a variant of NASA's Space Launch System,

was huge. Essentially a modern version of the Saturn V, its orange core stage tank was full of liquid fuel and flanked by two white solid fuel boosters like those used during the space shuttle program. With their Apollo-like Command Capsule and service module housed at the top, the whole apparatus stood more than 300 feet tall. It was the fourth time the rocket had been launched as part of their mission—the first three had been cargo launches, depositing the other components of their spacecraft into orbit for them to rendezvous with once they themselves were hurtling around the Earth. They were practically building a space station.

"Everyone okay?" The lead tech riding in the front passenger seat waited for all three crew members riding in the back to give him a verbal response before radioing their status back to launch control at nearby Patrick Air Force Base.

"Brown Eyes are a go," he said, referring to the crew's nickname, so-called because all three crew members had brown eyes. Given their varied African-American, Latino, and Jewish ethnicities, their shared eye color had quickly become a joke in the squadron, and one of the NASA advisers had made it official a few days earlier with a small plaque commemorating them as the "Brown Eyes" crew—the first manned mission crew of the newly-formed 3rd Expeditionary Space Squadron.

"Copy that," came the acknowledgement from Launch Control. Ground Control, listening in from the Buckley Air Force Base Annex in Colorado, also copied the status update.

The van drew closer to the launchpad, and Vicky and Jacob tilted their heads back farther and farther to see the top, while Derek leaned into the aisle to see out their windows.

"This is amazing," Jacob said as the sun rose, illuminating the rocket in pale golden light.

Vicky could only nod. Words couldn't express how she felt in that moment, and she silently catalogued the way the scene's incredible beauty made her chest ache, and how her stomach suddenly fluttered with nervous excitement at what they were about to do. In a matter of minutes, they'd be ascending the scaffolding to strap themselves to the top of a massive controlled explosion that would separate them from the planet. The whole thing was almost beyond comprehension.

The Brown Eyes crew had spent the better part of three years training for this mission—two years in NASA's astronaut candidate program, with slight variations to their schedules from those of the space agency's traditional candidates, and eight months at Air Force Space Command's brand new training facilities at the Buckley Annex where the 480th Space Expeditionary Wing was housed. Derek had been seconded to NASA already and had made two cargo runs to the International Space Station before joining the Air Force's new program, but for Jacob and Vicky, the mission would be a completely novel experience.

They'd trained as one of three mission crews selected from the original pool of candidates, but Vicky had started out on the Bravo Crew—the primary backups. Derek and Jacob had spent most of the months at Buckley training with a fellow Air Force officer, Major Kevin Thompson, who'd had to temporarily leave the program in the wake of a family emergency. Vicky had been bumped up to the primary crew just three weeks prior to launch. She was confident in her abilities, but the bonds Derek and Jacob had formed with Major Thompson over seven months of crew training were not easily replicated, and the reorganized crew were still getting to know each other.

The van parked near the launchpad and the crew and technicians disembarked. There was one tech for each crewmember, plus the lead tech, and they were the only people within five miles of the rocket. Together, the seven of them crowded into the tower elevator. Vicky checked the bun she'd pulled her brown hair into to make sure it was holding. Twenty-five stories up, the elevator came to a stop. Vicky looked down. She could see the van waiting below. Not far away, the Florida coastline met the Atlantic Ocean. It was a clear morning and the sky was already turning pale blue.

They made their way to the launch room, where the techs did their final suit checks for the crew. Then they all turned to the spacecraft. The lead tech went out first and Derek led the way for the crew, crawling forward across the platform connecting the elevator to the spacecraft, where the tech waited at the capsule door. He opened it as they approached and Derek crawled in, taking his seat on the left side of the capsule. Vicky scrambled in after him, sitting on the far right. Last came Jacob, who settled into the center seat. The techs helped them don their helmets and strapped them all in tightly.

No simulator had quite succeeded in mimicking how firmly they were now held in place. Jacob tried to shift in his discomfort, but he couldn't move his torso at all in the seat. His tech tapped on his helmet and he looked up. The man grinned and planted a big kiss on the plastic above Jacob's forehead.

"From your Mom!"

Jacob laughed and gave the tech a thumbs-up. He felt a slap on his shoulder, then the tech was gone. A moment later, the lead tech gave them a wave and the capsule door was shut. The crew was alone.

"Everybody alright?" Derek asked on the capsule's hot-miked internal radio system as he stored a note his tech had handed him safely into a pocket of his suit. It would be from his family. At forty-three, Derek was the oldest member of the crew by almost a decade, and had two grown children. Jacob was the youngest at twenty-nine, and neither he nor Vicky had families of their own. They were just young enough for Derek to feel a small sense of fatherly responsibility added to his role of Mission Commander.

"Good to go," Jacob replied.

"Squished but fine," Vicky said, making Jacob laugh again. She grinned at him, clutching a note of her own.

"*Pioneer*, this is Launch Control. Comm check."

Derek pressed his external radio switch to respond. "Launch Control, this is the *Pioneer*. We have you five by five."

"Copy that."

Vicky took a deep breath. The Command Capsule's call sign was a reminder of what they were doing. Not only would they be the first crew to be put in orbit by Air Force Space Command, they would also be going farther into space than anyone had ever gone before—much farther, if everything worked like it had in the two unmanned test flights the 480th Space Expeditionary Wing had launched in the previous year. As the crew's mission specialist, Vicky had little to do but confirm readings during the first stages of their mission. Her job wouldn't start in earnest until they had rendezvoused with the craft's other components and left Earth orbit, headed for Mars. Then they would begin running experiments and testing the new propulsion system, and Vicky would be in the hot seat.

Derek and Jacob started the preflight checklist. They had their comm check with Ground Control and turned on all the initial systems while the capsule was slowly pressurized.

"Approaching five minutes to launch."

"Roger, Launch Control."

"Mark."

"Mark," Derek said, setting the clock. The numbers clicked by, counting down, and he felt his heartrate tick up slightly. He pushed his excitement down. There was no guarantee they would launch. Something could go wrong, and the countdown would be aborted. They would climb out of the spacecraft and try again another day. But it was close now, and every second that ticked by increased the likelihood that they would soon be rocketing through the air toward outer space.

"Okay, *Pioneer*, let's start activating those final systems."

"Roger, Launch Control." Derek turned the page of his pre-flight checklist to the secondary pre-launch checklist. He tamped down another small surge of excitement and focused on his job. Two minutes went by as they powered up their final systems. Everything functioned as expected, and Derek began to think they just might launch.

"*Pioneer*, Launch Control. Do you have anything you'd like to say?"

It had been tradition for space shuttle crews to bid the Earth farewell just before launch, and the crew of the *Pioneer* had been told they would be expected to deliver a brief goodbye. It would be recorded for posterity, and broadcast live on Armed Forces Television. The Brown Eyes crew were prepared.

"Launch Control, this is the *Pioneer*. It is an honor and a privilege to be members of this unit and the Air Force's space superiority mission. This is a great undertaking and we are humbled to be a part of it."

He looked at Jacob, who took his cue.

"We would like to thank all the technicians, engineers, and support staff who've worked so hard to get us here. Your dedication has inspired each of us as we prepared for this mission."

Vicky keyed up her mic in turn. "We also want to thank our families and friends for their support during the months of training behind us, and the months of deployment ahead. We wouldn't be here without you. Over."

Derek nodded in the silence that followed Vicky's statement. Their coordinated speech had come off seamlessly.

"Roger that, *Pioneer*. Well said."

"Thank you, Launch Control."

"Prepare for final computer check."

"Roger," Derek said, and flipped to the final section of the pre-launch checklist. He and Jacob went through the list, confirming each step with Launch Control, and Vicky checked her own systems as far as possible. She would do her final checks when they rendezvoused with the module containing their new interplanetary propulsion system, or IPS—also known as the Hawking Engine—which she would control from her station.

"Clearing Caution and Warning memory," Jacob said, and pressed the associated icon on his touchscreen panel.

"Copy that, *Pioneer*. You're looking good."

The final checklist completed, the crew were left alone with their thoughts. Derek pulled the note out of his pocket and opened it. *Good luck, Dad! I love you!* was scribbled inside, in his daughter Theresa's handwriting. She would have written the note from dental hygiene school back home in Washington State. Underneath her message was one from his son Richard, who was following in his footsteps at the Air Force Academy: *Take care of yourself, Dad. See you when you're back Earthside.* Finally, he ran his fingers over lines of raised dots—his sister had written a message on her Brailler. *You have to tell me everything when you get back, ok? Love you.*

Derek smiled, thinking of the coordination and planning it had taken for all of them to use the same piece of paper. His sister must have been the last to sign it, and passed it on when she got to Florida to witness the launch. She'd be sitting in the stands five miles away with Jacob and Vicky's families, waiting to hear the rumble and blast of the rocket as it clawed its way through the air, and feel the vibrations it would create for miles around.

Derek glanced at the countdown: thirty-five seconds. He looked at all the buttons and switches and screens in front of him and felt his focus narrowing in on the task at hand, ready to respond in an instant should something go wrong. In the seat next to him, Jacob had stopped thinking about his mother and siblings in the viewing stands, and whether or not he would lose circulation from the tightness of the seat straps. He was now reviewing emergency abort procedures in his head. Vicky, on the far right, had tucked away the note from her family without reading it, and was going over every switch and button she might be called on to press in the event of an emergency during launch.

Seven seconds before launch, the main engines were successfully lit, and the rocket began to roar and pulse against its restraints. The countdown reached zero and the solid rocket boosters ignited. The entire spacecraft shuddered violently, shaking and rumbling as if it were about to rattle apart. The ground restraints detached and the rocket pushed off from the Earth. Derek looked out the window to his left and watched their progress as they accelerated past the launch tower.

"Tower cleared!" he shouted into his radio and heard the confirmation from Launch Control, the last communication they would share. His eyes shifted back to his readouts and he watched as they rose higher and higher through the air, looking for anything amiss, calculating a new emergency landing zone as each second took them out of range of the previous zone. The vehicle entered its roll program and turned to its target heading.

"Roll program, Ground," he said, marking the beginning of their communication with Ground Control, who would be their contact for the rest of the mission.

"Roger roll, *Pioneer*."

The ride grew steadily rougher as they fought their way through the air. Jacob grabbed a handle on his station and pulled himself forward with supreme effort, just to get his head off the back of the seat so his neck could absorb the vibration and he could focus his eyes on his instruments.

Vicky kept her eyes on the small window at her two o'clock. As they climbed, the light blue of the early-morning Florida sky grew darker. She saw it shift to indigo, and then suddenly it was black, and they were above the air.

"Booster jettison," came the command from Ground Control, and Derek flipped the switches. The solid rocket boosters detached with a burst of flame and dropped away.

"Booster jettison complete," Derek replied, louder than he intended in the relative quiet of their suddenly smooth ride. The minutes continued to tick by, and soon the crew had to work to breathe as their acceleration neared its peak.

"*Pioneer*, you are go for main engine separation."

"Roger," Derek said. He reached for the switch and flipped it. The core rocket stage detached behind them and began its fall to Earth. With the capsule no longer accelerating, the crew immediately became weightless.

"We have main engine sep," Derek said, his voice tinged with laughter at the feeling. Jacob started outright giggling and even Vicky was laughing at the ridiculous way her arms floated in the air without effort.

"Roger, *Pioneer*. You are looking good."

"Mission Stage One complete," Derek said to himself, and looked out at the miraculous Earth speeding by.

CHAPTER TWO

Six days later, the crew was still marveling at the feeling of weightlessness, even as they pushed ahead with their duties as if it were all business as usual.

Derek keyed up the external mic. "Ground, *Pioneer*. We're just about ready for our final docking maneuvers."

"Copy." Colonel Liz Fischer's voice came over the radio. As the Bravo Crew commander, Vicky had trained closely with her for seven months before being pulled to the Alpha Crew. Vicky sighed. She wished her friend and colleague was there with them.

The Brown Eyes crew was sitting strapped in to their seats so that they wouldn't float around too much, comfortable in their green flight suits. They'd already rendezvoused with two of the spacecraft's three additional components, following a day of system checks to make sure everything in the Command Capsule was working and to allow them time to adjust to weightlessness. After their initial childlike glee, they'd all been nauseated for a while. Vicky thought she'd seen Jacob throwing a barf bag into the trash, but she hadn't asked and he hadn't volunteered anything. Now their bodies had adjusted to the strangeness of it all and they were building their ship.

The Command Capsule had been attached to a large service module when they launched, containing an engine, fuel cells, batteries, and oxygen and water tanks, as well as thrusters, a communications array, solar panels for recharging the batteries, and cooling panels for radiating excess heat away from the spacecraft.

Once they had established orbit, they had deployed the solar and cooling panels and docked with their Habitat Module, a compact living area, laboratory, gym and storage facility complete with airlock should they need to effect any repairs to the ship's exterior on their way to or from Mars. After the habitat they'd docked with the Hawking Engine, which would allow them to fly to Mars in just sixty-eight days on this first manned test flight. Now they were ready to dock with their final component, the Mars Storage Module, or MSM. The smallest part of the ship after the Command Capsule, the MSM held containers of oxygen, water, and other necessities, to stock the planet for future manned missions to the surface. It was a payload NASA had requested they drop off at the red planet as part of their Martian exploration research. In addition, there was a passive entangled particles experiment DARPA and MIT were using to test the distance limits of entanglement. Nothing in the MSM would be accessible to them during the flight to Mars, but it was an important part of their mission nonetheless.

Vicky kept her eye on the feed from a camera placed near the front of the Hawking Engine. Since each new component of the spacecraft docked at the front of the previous one, the only docking maneuver Derek had performed with the naked eye was the first one. After that, he'd relied on the pre-positioned cameras at the front of each additional module to successfully dock with the next. It was delicate, focused work. As the mission pilot, Derek had control of their ship, and as navigator, Jacob backed him up with velocity and attitude information. Once they'd docked with the MSM, Vicky would power up the Habitat Module and inspect it as Derek and Jacob prepared to leave Earth's orbit.

The back edge of the MSM slid closer and out of the camera's line of sight. Vicky held her breath. They'd practiced each of these dockings in simulators, but it felt different to Vicky now that it was actually happening.

Derek let out a low breath.

"Looking good," Jacob said quietly.

Vicky felt a tremor in the spacecraft. Several indicators lit up in green on Vicky's side of the capsule.

"Instrumentation looks good, Colonel," she said. "All systems green."

"Alright," Derek said, and keyed up his mic. "Ground, we have docked with the MSM. All green, over."

"Copy. We're seeing that as well. Good job."

"What's our timeline?" Derek asked, having lost track as he focused solely on maneuvering the spacecraft for rendezvous.

"You've got about five hours, *Pioneer*."

"Roger."

Now that the spacecraft was complete, they needed to power up the Habitat Module and double-check their systems and supply readings before leaving Earth's orbit.

"Alright, Mendez, let's get started on that checklist," Derek said as Vicky unstrapped herself. "Abrams, don't forget to wait for my okay."

"I won't," Vicky said, pushing aside a flutter of annoyance. Derek and Jacob had to make sure the habitat was fully pressurized equal to the pressurization of the capsule before she went in and started powering things up, and they had simulated this moment a dozen times—she didn't need to be told. But he was only doing his job and reminding her, just in case, she told herself. It wasn't because he didn't trust her. It wasn't because she was still "new." He was just the kind of guy who liked to be thorough.

Vicky maneuvered to the hatch that stood between them and the habitat and held herself in place using a small handle on the side of the capsule, where she waited.

"Okay, Abrams," Derek finally said, and Vicky opened the hatch. She stowed it in its compartment under her seat and grabbed her flashlight from the pocket on the right leg of her flight suit.

It was dark and cold inside the cylindrical Habitat Module when Vicky propelled herself lightly through the access tunnel. She found the button for the emergency lights and pressed it. The habitat flooded with dim white light. Vicky smiled, turning off her flashlight and stowing it in her pocket before moving to the control panel a few inches away, where she hooked the grooves of her specialized socks into the floor to steady herself as she opened the power-up display and started going through the checklist that hung next to the screen. It would take her about two hours to fully power up the habitat, and another hour to inspect it to make sure everything was in order. Then they'd be set.

The Habitat Module was a state-of-the-art piece of equipment, a little bigger than the pressurized modules on the International Space Station. On the right side going down from the access tunnel, there was a semi-circular table the crew would use for work and dining, with a bench seat wrapped around it that they could strap themselves into or float around with their feet anchored to the grooves in the floor. Beyond the table was their food storage and hot and cold water taps, an area affectionately called the kitchen. Beyond that was their toilet facility and a small separate bathroom space for cleaning their skin and hair. There was even a compact, dry-cleaning-like machine for their clothing that had been invented through DARPA for the mission so they wouldn't need to bring as much with them.

The left side of the module began with laboratory space. The *Pioneer* was carrying several experiments onboard that they would be responsible for running during their months-long mission. There was a soft matter experiment for DARPA involving the formation of crystals, a new laser that the Air Force wanted tested in space, and two experiments that NASA had asked them to run: a biological experiment revolving around photosynthesis, and a human research experiment studying the effects of long-term travel through deep space on their own samples and biometric data. Finally, there was the bubble counter. Vials of a special gel were set up in various places around the Command Capsule and the habitat. When radioactive particles came through the sides of the ship, they left tiny bubbles in the gel. Every day, the vials would be collected and put into the bubble counter, a machine that literally counted the bubbles and kept the crew informed about the effectiveness of the ship's shielding against radiation.

The "gym" came next, consisting of a fold-down tread-

mill with restraining straps to hold them down so they
could run with simulated gravitational pull, and several
bands and other resistance training tools to minimize the
damage to their skeletons and muscles on the long voyage.
A tiny bedroom followed the gym, equipped with a verti-
cally situated sleep sack for the crewmembers to take turns
zipping themselves into to hold them stationary while they
slept, which Vicky was looking forward to after nearly a
week trying to sleep in the cramped Command Capsule.

Finally, just before the airlock, there was a large locker
containing a spacesuit for each astronaut in case they had
to conduct a spacewalk. Each suit had been custom made
for each astronaut, with a little over an inch of extra height
in anticipation of how their spines would lengthen without the pressure of gravity to keep them compressed. The
suits were standard NASA EMUs. Vicky could remember
when the group of astronaut candidates were first intro-
duced to the suits during their astronaut candidate training
at NASA—they'd called them individual spaceships, and
they really were. The candidates had complete a variety of
training activities while wearing the suits underwater, with
no issues. Still, everyone hoped they could get through the
mission without needing the suits– spacewalking was a
dangerous activity. No matter how well designed the suits
were or how meticulously the spacewalk was planned, exiting the ship left them vulnerable. The suits were not as well
fortified as the reinforced sides of their spacecraft, and they
only carried a nine-hour reserve of oxygen; if something
went wrong on a spacewalk, it could go very wrong, very
quickly.

When she completed the power-up, Vicky made the

rounds, inspecting everything on board and setting up their experiments. All three of them were trained to run the experiments, but it was primarily Vicky's job as the mission specialist.

"How's it going in there?"

Vicky suppressed another tug of irritation at her mission commander's question, called out from the Command Capsule. He and Jacob had obviously finished their checklists and any housekeeping procedures Ground Control may have asked them to do. Vicky sternly told herself not to be touchy—he was just checking in.

"Almost done, sir!" she called back. She took a breath before continuing with her inspection. They'd been training together for three weeks, and she thought she had adjusted to her new crewmembers' idiosyncrasies, but it was taking her longer than she'd expected to get used to Derek's hands-on leadership style; Liz would've let her work in peace until she showed back up in the crew capsule or radioed from the habitat that she was finished. Derek didn't micromanage, but he liked to touch base a lot more, at least with Vicky. She wasn't sure he did that as much with Jacob, but she couldn't be sure; they did spend most of their time working together in the crew capsule.

Vicky felt a pang of loneliness to go with her insecurity and rolled her eyes at herself as she did her final check of the airlock. She had a PhD in accelerator physics and several years of work experience under her belt before she'd been approached for this new Air Force program. She had done well in training, too. The Bravo Crew navigator, Major Paul Brightman, had told her more than once that he enjoyed working with her and was surprised she hadn't been assigned to the Alpha Crew from the beginning, words Vicky was grateful for now as she reminded herself that she was perfectly competent, no matter what crew she was put with. Still, her confidence fluttered uncertainly in the face of being the new kid.

Vicky squared her shoulders. She'd just have to deal with it.

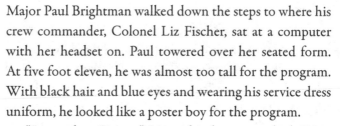

Major Paul Brightman walked down the steps to where his crew commander, Colonel Liz Fischer, sat at a computer with her headset on. Paul towered over her seated form. At five foot eleven, he was almost too tall for the program. With black hair and blue eyes and wearing his service dress uniform, he looked like a poster boy for the program.

"Roger that, *Pioneer*," Liz said as he approached. "Hey, Paul. How are you?"

"Doing well, Colonel," he answered. "How have things been?"

"Quiet. They've successfully docked with all their component modules and have powered up the habitat. Vicky finished her inspection over an hour ago, so they're ready to go. They're just waiting for their scheduled window."

"Great," Paul said, taking the seat as Liz vacated it and smoothed the wrinkles out of her own dress uniform. He set his coffee on the tabletop surface a safe distance from the keyboard and opened his headset case.

"Everything's gone smoothly so far," Liz continued to update him. "All three dockings were completed without any problems."

"That's good," Paul said, smiling at her. At five foot two, Liz was the shortest astronaut in the program, but she never seemed like it. She had an easy confidence that often gave the impression that she was the tallest person in the room.

"You've still got a few minutes before your shift," she said, looking at her watch.

"That's okay," Paul replied. "What else am I going to do here?" He plugged in his headset and put it on his head, adjusting the mic so it hovered near his lips.

"You set?"

"Yep. *Pioneer*, Ground. Comm check," he said, keying up the mic to talk to the crew in orbit.

"We read you, Ground, and Abrams says hi," came Colonel Derek Williams' voice through some mild static.

Paul grinned. The Bravo Crew had become a little family during their months of dedicated crew training, and Paul and Vicky had developed a sibling-like relationship. He was happy she'd gotten a shot at the first launch, but he missed her.

"Hello to Vicky," he answered simply.

"Alright," Liz said, unplugging her headset. "I'll leave you to it." She gathered up her things and headed out with a final nod "goodbye."

"Bye." Paul swiveled in his seat to take in Ground Control. Each member of the three astronaut crews had trained in the position of Crewcom, or Crew Communications. It was the Air Force's take on NASA's "CapCom," and Paul didn't see why they had to rename the position just because they weren't NASA. He could even see their NASA adviser from his seat. She was standing next to the spaceflight supervisor—again a position renamed for the

Air Force instead of using NASA's "flight director"—with her headset plugged in. Technically, training was over and the spaceflight supervisors were all fully qualified, but their advisors were putting their time to good use, shadowing and advising the three alternating spaceflight supervisors for their first few days.

Like NASA's flight director, the spaceflight supervisor had complete decision-making authority in Ground Control, no matter who outranked him. Lieutenant Colonel Jeff Marshall was the supervisor on duty, having come in a few minutes before Paul for the shift change. He was a short, wiry man with rapidly graying brown hair and an air of competent experience. Paul always enjoyed working shift when Jeff was on duty—if the Bravo Crew had their full complement, their alternating shifts would have him on duty every time Jeff was for consistency, but until Major Thompson returned, they were a man short and Paul and Liz were alternating every two shifts to the spaceflight supervisors' three.

Paul turned his attention to the rest of the room as Jeff prompted the various stations to check in with updates now that the shift change had occurred. The stations were manned with officers and enlisted personnel, and here and there a civilian contractor with prior experience at NASA's Mission Control. It was an intense place to work, Paul mused as he swiveled, and the pressure was on for their first manned flight. He appreciated the expertise and bearing of everyone there, especially those in the junior ranks, both officer and enlisted—they were young, but their professionalism and competence were extremely gratifying. When it was Paul's turn to launch, Ground Control's ability to function at the highest level was one thing he wouldn't have to worry about.

The static picked up in his headset, signaling that the crew was about to speak. "Ground, *Pioneer*."

"Yeah, go ahead, *Pioneer*," Paul said, sitting up and stopping the movement of his chair. Everyone in the room seemed to pause mid-breath to listen in—they had heard the static, too.

"We are ready to begin Mars ingress."

Paul glanced at Colonel Marshall, who held up his finger in a "wait" signal.

"Roger that, *Pioneer*," Paul said into the mic. "Standby."

"*Pioneer* standing by."

A minute passed, and then another, as Colonel Marshall checked on their timeline and conferred with the airmen working the Navigation station, which was in charge of the *Pioneer*'s flight path to and from Mars. Finally, Colonel Marshall looked back over at Paul.

"Crewcom, this is Flight."

"Go, Flight," Paul said, trying not to sound too eager.

"They're good to go. Tell them to proceed."

"Roger that. *Pioneer*, Ground, you have a go for Mars ingress."

"Copy. Leaving Earth orbit."

Paul shook his head at the incongruence of Derek's indifferent tone and what was about to happen. They were all making history, and they were all just doing their jobs.

CHAPTER THREE

Two days into the cruise, they began engine tests. Since they had left Earth orbit, the crew had been taking care of housekeeping procedures, checking and running experiments, and generally settling in for the long haul. They'd conducted a few tests to check the IPS—everything short of actually engaging the engine. Now they were ready to begin their first manned functional test of the Hawking Engine.

A breakthrough in both accelerator physics and space-flight propulsion, the Hawking Engine was essentially a compact particle accelerator running in reverse time. Superconducting magnets captured the random fluctuations of space-time and divided it into separate, stable streams of charged matter and anti-matter, like Maxwell's demon run amok. The matter was directed out in every direction except the fore and aft of the engine apparatus, diffused into the surrounding empty space evenly so as not to send them off-course in any given direction. The anti-matter, meanwhile, was directed toward the aft of the spacecraft. This artificially generated Hawking Radiation propelled the ship forward without the requirement of large amounts of additional fuel—the engine ran on solar power picked up from the sun via the large solar panels on the service module.

The Air Force had already conducted successful unmanned test flights with the engine, first via the unmanned X-37 Orbital Test Vehicle, and then with an unmanned version of the Orion capsule system. As the first manned flight with the Hawking Engine, the *Pioneer* crew had to run additional tests on their way to Mars, and would not be pushing their engine to maximum capability for an extended period of time. Theirs would be the first of many flights that would pave the way for NASA's manned missions to Mars by cutting the ingress and egress to a fraction of the three years it would take astronauts to get there and back using conventional propulsion systems. This was why NASA had worked so closely with the Air Force's Space Command on the project.

"Okay, *Pioneer*," came Paul's voice over the radio. "You are a go for IPS test, phase one."

"Roger that," Derek replied. "Alright, Abrams, you know the drill. Engage the Hawk-E at five percent efficiency."

"Five percent," Vicky confirmed, silently thinking there was no need for his "you know the drill" commentary. They had already run through the pre-test checklist and all that was left for her to do was input the percentage and hit the icon on her touchscreen. There was a small lurch as the engine came online, but it smoothed right out. The crew only felt a slight amount of pressure as the acceleration reminded them that they weren't actually weightless, but had only felt that way without the effects of gravity.

"Engine at five percent capacity." Vicky scanned the screen in front of her. "Three green," she said, referring to the status lights on her readout. Green was good. Yellow indicated an error or other issue, and red was the failure warning. No light at all meant no functionality.

"Power looks good," Derek said.

"We're maintaining attitude." Jacob added. He glanced out the window directly above him to visually confirm by the stars that they were staying on course before checking their acceleration. "G-Force of point one two."

"Roger. Ground, *Pioneer*, we are at five percent. Everything looks good on our end."

"Copy that. It looks good here, as well. Go ahead and increase to ten percent."

"Ten percent," Derek repeated by way of acknowledgement and Vicky made the change, the computer automatically increasing their acceleration gradually until they hit the ten percent mark.

"We're at ten percent—five green," Vicky said, and Derek relayed to Ground Control.

"Still good on attitude," Jacob reported. "G-force point two three."

"Ground, we're at ten percent and no problems," Derek said.

"Ok, *Pioneer*, we'll hold for now as planned. Standby for follow-up."

"*Pioneer* standing by."

The crew relaxed a little. Ground Control would be checking all their data to make sure everything was running as it should be, but the lack of Caution and Warning lights and alarms in the Command Capsule boded well for the test. They did what they could to check everything on their end, and found nothing that varied from normal parameters. Jacob took a couple of aspirin for a headache. He unhooked his feet from the floor experimentally and chuckled as he had to work a little to move his leg now that they were experiencing some G-forces, however minor, as they continued to accelerate at ten percent of the Hawking Engine's capability.

Vicky smiled tightly at him when he nudged her. They weren't actively working but the middle of a systems test didn't strike her as a good time to play around. She was just thinking Colonel Williams should say something to the captain when Jacob voluntarily re-anchored his feet.

"Oh, come on, Vicky," he said. "Lighten up a little. We can't do anything until they get back to us."

"At which point I'll need to be ready to act," Vicky countered calmly. There was a slight archness to her voice that she couldn't quite help, though, and Jacob noticed it. He opened his mouth to respond but Derek had followed the interplay and decided to cut him off.

"Alright, that's enough. You could do with a little sobering up, yourself, Mendez—maybe you'll be a good influence on each other."

He successfully hid his amusement when both of his young crewmates stared at him in a mixture of surprise and doubt. Jacob and Vicky had rubbed each other the wrong way a few times during their three weeks of pre-launch crew training. Nothing serious, of course—they were all professionals. But they had very different personalities and approaches to a problem and they hadn't ironed out all their interpersonal kinks yet. Derek could have let them have a moment of friction, but Vicky was right that they needed to stay focused and ready to act. They had months of spaceflight ahead of them; at this point, Derek thought it better to diffuse any possible situations before they became real issues rather than having to do damage control after the fact.

He knew from the last eight months of working closely with Jacob that a firm hand with light overtones was an effective method of curtailing the captain's enthusiasm when it ran a little high, but he still wasn't sure what leadership methods were most effective with Vicky. He took in her return to a businesslike demeanor as she rechecked a few systems that didn't need rechecking. She had a slight flush in her cheeks and he wasn't sure if it was from Jacob's ribbing or her being included in the mild reprimand, but he put the thought away for another time. It was early days, and a particularly stressful one for Vicky. Derek had found her surprisingly well-adapted to the rigidity of the Air Force chain of command, and the knowledge that she took orders quietly had done much to help him agree with the idea of putting her on the crew when Major Thompson had left.

Jacob, meanwhile, had also subsided and was fiddling with his half-sheet notebook. They each had one in addition to all the required checklists—a spiral-bound book filled with personalized notes on anything they may each be required to do during the mission, with digital backups in the onboard computer and each crewmember's personal laptop. Jacob looked pensive. He'd been headachy lately and Derek suspected that, out of the three of them, Jacob was having the most trouble sleeping.

Derek sighed and looked out his window. He had complete confidence in the preparedness and abilities of his crewmates. He just wasn't sure how well they'd all get along for the next six and a half months in close quarters on a stressful mission. He thought of his sister's exhortation to tell her everything when they got back. There would certainly be plenty of unclassified stories to tell, and his teammates' antics would be at the top of the list. The thought made him smirk a little as he checked the onboard atomic clock. Just a few more minutes and they'd be increasing the IPS engagement to fifteen percent.

"What have you got, IPS?" Colonel Jeff Marshall stood and looked toward the IPS station. A senior airman and a civilian were seated in front of a bank of computers, and the airman swiveled around halfway to be able to make eye contact.

"We're seeing an irregular reading on the Hawk-E, Sir," the airman said. "The angle on main mag nine is reading skewed by negative point two percent. That's within our margin of error, so it's not triggering a Caution and Warning in the Command Capsule, but it is possible the magnet could actually be off alignment."

Jeff nodded his understanding. The flow of matter and anti-matter from the Hawking Engine was controlled by a series of magnets. The primary magnets were called main mags, and controlled several sub-magnet series. They all worked together to ensure the proper acceleration and directional flow of particles in the engine. If any of the magnets came out of alignment by too great a percentage, it could cause major problems, including rendering the engine inert.

"Alright," he said. "Thanks for bringing it to my attention. Let me know if there's any change."

"Yes, sir," the airman said, and swiveled back around to face the screens.

Jeff found himself glancing toward Paul Brightman on Crewcom, but the major didn't say anything. He was looking at the colonel, ready if Jeff wanted him to notify the crew, but Jeff could tell by his posture that he wasn't expecting that to be the case, and he was right. If the reading was within their margin of error, there was no sense telling the crew and pulling their focus away from their jobs. Jeff shook his head and Paul acknowledged it with a nod. The colonel looked down at his typed notes. Now that IPS had given their report, he received updates from everyone. Once every department had reported in, he keyed up his mic again.

"Crewcom, Flight," he said.

"Go, Flight," Paul responded immediately, turning again to make eye contact.

"Go ahead and report all systems go. We'll continue at this rate of acceleration for the rest of the half-hour as planned before shutting down the engine and coasting."

"Roger." Paul turned back to his position and keyed his mic for long range communications. "*Pioneer*, Ground," he said crisply.

"Go ahead, Ground," Colonel Williams said a bit later, his reply already delayed by the distance the signal had to travel.

"Status is green, all systems go," Paul said. "Continue acceleration at ten percent IPS engagement until 1032 Zulu, then commence with IPS shutdown."

"Roger that," came the slightly garbled voice. "Continue

at ten percent until IPS shutdown at 1032 Zulu."

"Flight?" The young airman first class working the Link station spoke up as soon as Derek was finished.

"Yeah, have them change to omni bravo," Jeff said, anticipating the requested change in radio systems when he heard the static on the transmission.

"Thanks, Flight," the airman said quickly.

"*Pioneer*, go ahead and change to omni bravo," Paul said.

"Omni bravo," came the reply. They all waited for a few moments, then Derek's voice came over the radio again, clearer and stronger.

"Ground, *Pioneer*, comm check."

"Five by five, *Pioneer*," Paul said, letting Derek know they could hear him loud and clear.

"Roger," Derek replied, and the radio fell silent.

The flight surgeon approached Jeff's position. "Sir, Captain Mendez's temperature is still a little high."

"What is it?"

"100.2 degrees."

"That's hardly a fever," Jeff pointed out.

"No, but it's been there for the last two days, give or take a tenth of a degree, and I don't want it going up. I'd like him to get a little extra rest, just in case."

"Okay," Jeff agreed, and scribbled a note for himself on a pad of paper on his desk. "As soon as they've shut off the IPS we'll relay that."

"Thank you, sir."

A slightly raised temperature and a quirky magnet reading. Jeff nodded to himself. If those were the only problems they encountered during the mission, they'd be extremely lucky.

Paul leaned back in his chair to stretch his legs out a bit more. He listened to the quiet hum of occasional chatter over his headset from various elements of Ground Control communicating with each other as they analyzed the steady stream of near-real-time data coming over the downlink from the *Pioneer*'s Command Capsule. Paul smiled to himself even as he listened and checked his computer for relevant chat room activity. Of all the career paths he had ever thought of pursuing, he never thought he'd be an astronaut in the Air Force's first manned spaceflight program. Whether there on Earth acting as the liaison between Ground Control and the crew of the *Pioneer*, or up in space himself, it was incredible no matter what way he looked at it. There were only nine of them: three in space, three at Buckley, including the still-absent Major Thompson, and the three members of Charlie Crew, who'd flown to Australia ahead of the launch so they could communicate with the *Pioneer* while the Earth spun on its axis and the ship moved in its every-expanding orbit around the sun on its way to Mars. It was, Paul thought, the best job in the world. And he was doing it.

Paul sat up straight as Derek's voice came through his headset again.

"Ground, *Pioneer*."

"Go ahead, *Pioneer*."

"After IPS cutoff, we're still set to coast for twenty-four hours, correct?"

"That's affirm," Paul said.

"We'd like to rearrange the sleep schedule for that period, if we could. I recommend Mendez takes first sleep shift and gets two extra hours, taking an hour each from myself and Abrams."

Jeff chuckled as the flight surgeon's head swiveled toward Paul, his face creased in concern.

"FAO?" Jeff asked on his headset.

"That's fine, Flight," the young lieutenant at the Flight Activities Officer station said.

Jeff gave Paul the nod.

"Uh, *Pioneer*, Ground. Yeah, that's not a problem. We're making a note. Is Captain Mendez alright?"

"He's fine," Derek said. "Just a little fatigued."

"Roger."

Paul shrugged, a gesture meant for both Jeff and the flight surgeon, who frowned but turned back to his medical readouts of the crew's biometric data.

Jeff hid a smile. He should have known the crew would sort things out for themselves. He scratched out the note he'd made to talk to them about giving Mendez more time to sleep once the test was over. He wondered momentarily if they'd gotten the whole truth from Colonel Williams, but immediately put the doubt out of his mind. He wasn't worried; if Mendez was experiencing anything more than mild fatigue, Derek would have said so. Hopefully the extra hours of rest would do the trick and he'd be back to his normal self. If not, they could add one more problem to the short list of things that hadn't gone perfectly, and that was only to be expected. They were sending people to Mars on an experimental spacecraft, after all. Nobody was expecting a perfect mission.

Across the aisle, Paul was swiveling thoughtfully in his chair. Jacob was not the macho type, but he would still hate to appear to be the weak link among the crew. From the crew's reports, he'd been the most nauseous after launch and had taken the longest to recover and adjust to weight-lessness. He hoped the captain wasn't worrying about it. Those were physiological reactions that just couldn't be controlled, no matter how healthy and fit a person was. Paul figured Jacob's fatigue was down to the fact that they hadn't had much downtime in the mission yet; he hadn't had time to recuperate from those initial symptoms.

Paul smiled sheepishly. He himself had been sick the first time they went on the Vomit Comet—the parabolic flights that allowed them to experience brief periods of weightlessness during their astronaut training. Jacob had been in his group, and had teased him mercilessly for weeks. Even Vicky, normally Paul's staunchest ally, had laughed about it. If he were a little less professional or cared a little less about his fellow navigator, Paul might have returned the favor right then. But they weren't having dinner at the end of a day of training—Jacob was actually in space during a stressful phase of an active mission. So instead of making a comment right then, Paul made a mental note to prepare some good teasing material for a more relaxed time. He owed Jacob some good-humored humiliation.

CHAPTER FOUR

"Guess what, everyone?"

Vicky and Derek twisted in their seats as Jacob emerged from the access tunnel that connected the Command Capsule to the Habitat Module, sounding frustrated. He didn't wait for them to respond.

"I have a cold sore."

Vicky frowned but Derek turned back around to hide a smile.

"Cold sore?" Vicky asked.

"Yep," Jacob said in the same tone as before, taking his seat. "A cold sore. I hate that stupid herpes virus."

"Well, they did say we could experience virus reactivation," Vicky said sympathetically.

"Yeah, I know," Jacob said, strapping himself in. "'Certain viruses that lie dormant in the body can reactivate under stress,'" he said, quoting the flight surgeon.

"'And space is a very stressful place,'" Derek finished for him.

Vicky realized she had leaned away from Jacob as he'd settled in, and forced herself to re-center in her seat.

"When's the last time you had them?" she asked, hoping he hadn't noticed.

"I think I was twelve years old," he said. "I haven't had so much as a canker sore since then and now they're back."

"I guess that extra sleep didn't do much for you, then," Derek said, allowing a little dry humor into his voice.

Jacob looked at him suspiciously. "No," he said. "Apparently not. Not that I actually slept much." He tightened his seatbelt. "Let's just get this over with."

Vicky and Derek's gaze collided across the capsule and Vicky had to press her lips together and look away to avoid laughing at the amusement she saw in Derek's eyes. Jacob was tired and not feeling well; he was cranky. Somehow she didn't think he'd appreciate being openly laughed at.

"You ready, Abrams?" Derek asked, his voice even and businesslike.

"Ready, sir," she said, matching his tone.

"Okay. Ground, *Pioneer*. We are ready for IPS test, phase two." They waited in silence for a few minutes, each crewmember busy running final system checks until they received their reply.

"Roger, *Pioneer*. Engage Hawk-E at five percent."

"Engaging IPS."

They followed the same procedure as before, pausing at ten percent throttle to give Ground Control time to receive and analyze all the data the ship was sending them. Then they got the go-ahead to increase to fifteen percent, then twenty, and finally twenty-five, where they would hold for half an hour before shutting off the engine to coast for another day of checking their vitals, running the onboard experiments, and resting. Part of the purpose of their mission was to study the effect of prolonged G-forces and frequent changes in G-forces on the human body, so they were taking samples and completing surveys after each round of acceleration and return to weightlessness. They'd work their way up to one hundred percent acceleration, which would see them experiencing 2.3g. It wasn't much, but they would sustain that for about an hour. Once they shut the IPS off and stopped accelerating, they would coast until it was time to use the IPS in reverse to slow themselves back down in preparation for entering Mars orbit.

"*Pioneer*, Ground, shut off IPS."

The crew looked at each other in surprise. They'd only been running at twenty-five percent for a few minutes.

"Shut it off," Derek said quickly, knowing that with the time delay, they were already a few minutes behind the order.

"Shutting off IPS," Vicky said, and swiftly went through the five-step shutdown sequence while Derek answered Ground Control.

"Ground, *Pioneer*, we are shutting off the IPS. Any reason we cut the test short? Over."

"IPS is off."

"Everything looks fine on my end," Jacob said, checking their attitude and his navigational system.

"Everything's fine here too. It's got to be something to do with the engine itself," Derek said. "Abrams?"

"Just a second," Vicky said. She moved from screen to screen on the display in front of her, looking for anything unusual, but there was no sign of a problem.

"Everything looks fine," she said. "Must be something they saw in the detailed data."

Derek sighed. They'd been experiencing ever-increasing delays in their comms as they moved farther and farther from Earth. Ground Control probably hadn't received their message yet, let alone sent a reply. All they could do was wait.

"Any ideas?" Derek asked.

Vicky realized that both men were looking at her. She pushed aside a frisson of irritation at their assumption that she would have a solution to a problem they couldn't even identify. "If it's the Hawk-E it isn't showing up on my system. So it could just be a precaution they're taking with some abnormal readings that aren't strong enough to trip a Caution and Warning."

"Or we could have an instrumentation problem," Jacob said. "Maybe it is strong enough for Caution and Warning but there's something wrong with the system and it didn't trip like it should have."

"Or," Vicky said, not meaning to argue but finding herself doing it anyway, "maybe they didn't like something else they were seeing. Like some sort of stress on the ship, or maybe our bio readings."

"I feel fine," Jacob said.

"Besides your cold sore?"

Derek raised his eyebrows at Vicky in surprise at her aggressive tone. She blushed and looked away.

"Sorry," she murmured.

Jacob glared at Vicky for a moment longer. "Yes," he said irritably. "Besides my cold sore."

"*Pioneer*, Ground. We're just double-checking some data. Over."

"Roger," Derek said, wondering what they weren't being told. "*Pioneer* standing by."

Jacob pressed his head against the back of his seat and

sighed. All this speeding up and slowing back down to zero gravity was actually making his stomach uneasy, but he wasn't about to say so after Vicky's comment. The symptoms were only lasting a few minutes each time, so he figured he'd ride it out in silence. He didn't feel well enough to joke about it, anyway.

The three of them waited in their seats for almost half an hour before they heard back from Ground Control.

"*Pioneer*, Ground. We'd like you to do a main mag alignment reset and run a full check on the IPS, over."

"Uh, copy main mag realign. Stand by."

Derek glanced across the capsule at Vicky to gauge her response to the unexpected request, but she wasn't looking at him. She was already working on the alignment reset procedure in her checklist, frowning in concentration. These kinds of procedures fell into the "troubleshooting" category, but if Ground Control was seeing something in their data to raise concerns that a magnet was not aligned correctly, there could be a number of problems, ranging from a false reading all the way to a catastrophic failure of the Hawking Engine that could threaten the mission.

Vicky flipped the final switch and imagined the *clunk* they would hear if they weren't in a vacuum, as the magnets were mechanically jostled to ensure that they were properly seated in their designated slots. She counted to sixty in her head, then started to run a new system check, just like they'd done after leaving Earth orbit before they began their tests on the Hawking Engine. She went through each step carefully, checking for any indications of a problem, and found none.

"Everything looks good to go," she said finally. "Whatever they're seeing on their end, I definitely don't have any indicators here."

"Alright. Ground, we have realigned the main magnets and run our checks. All systems are a go. Over."

Jacob sighed again in the middle seat as they waited for Ground Control's response.

"You okay?" Vicky asked softly. She felt bad for snapping at him earlier, when she knew he wasn't feeling well. Maybe the lack of sleep was starting to affect her too—it was almost impossible to sleep soundly in zero gravity.

Jacob took the olive branch with an understanding smile. "Yeah, just a little tired. Still."

"Well," she said, "I don't know about you, but all this stop-and-go is making me a little nauseated."

"Oh, yeah?" Jacob asked, perking up. "Where are you on the Garn scale?"

Vicky rolled her eyes at his reference to NASA's very unofficial nausea scale. "Not bad," she said. "Maybe two Garns each time we shut off the IPS."

"Mmm. I'm clocking in at three point five," Jacob said. "What about you, sir?"

"I don't get nauseous," Derek said smoothly, glad to see some of Jacob's customary humor returning.

"What about after launch? I was at Garn six, I think."

"Actual vomit?"

"I didn't see it happen," Vicky said with mock skepticism.

"I hid in the bathroom," Jacob confided in a loud stage whisper, and Vicky couldn't quite hold back an amused smirk. To their left, Derek grunted his own playful doubts of Jacob's honesty.

"I did! I felt it coming on, and I—"

"*Pioneer*, you are go for IPS retest, starting at five percent. Proceed when ready."

"You're on, Abrams."

"Yes, sir." Vicky programmed in the numbers and double-checked the system to make sure nothing looked off. Now that it was time to run another test, she could feel the nerves returning, especially since something had looked fishy enough to Ground Control for them to request a magnet reset. Of course, they may have been being overly cautious, but spaceflight supervisors had to weigh the value of the mission against the possibility of a catastrophic failure—which was basically anything that could lead to a shift in mission objectives or an aborted mission, all the way up to a loss of life onboard the spacecraft. Before they launched, the simulations team had calculated a total of at least six hundred and fifty catastrophic failures with potential to occur during their flight. If the likelihood of each weren't so small, they would never have launched.

"Okay, I'm all set," she said.

"Go ahead."

Vicky began the test anew. The crew waited tensely at each step, ready in case they received a call from Ground Control to shut down the IPS. Instead, they were given the go-ahead to increase the engine capacity to ten percent, then fifteen, and then twenty. They waited for the go-ahead to increase to twenty-five percent, but the expected call did not come when it should have. Derek checked the clock. Even with the ever-increasing time delay, they should have heard from Ground Control, with instructions to either continue the test or abort it. He automatically started mentally reviewing all the reasons there might be an extra delay in hearing from Ground Control, even as he grabbed his notebook and started checking his calculations for the expected time delay.

In the right seat, Vicky had also taken note of the prolonged radio silence. She debated whether she should say anything until she saw what Derek was doing. It made sense that if she'd noticed the unexpected quiet that he had too—he was the mission commander, after all, and the only one of them who'd been in space before. If anyone was going to notice something unexpected, it was him. Vicky tried to relax a little with the thought that he would also know what to do. They'd all trained for loss of communication with Ground, and there could be a variety of reasons for the disruption. Still, even an expected disruption in comms would create tension at home and in space until they reestablished link. This unexpected disruption had Vicky's heart beating faster in her chest as the possible implications flooded her mind. She forced herself to take a couple of deep breaths and willed her pulse to go back to normal.

Jacob had yet to notice the silence on the radio or the tension in the capsule. He was looking up out his window, completely focused on the position of the constellation Orion, which he'd been using as his primary visual reference ever since they'd gotten on course for Mars intercept. The constellation was clearly visible out his large navigational window, the bright stars of Orion's belt forming a reliable touchstone by its position within the window frame, but he could swear that line had shifted a little since the last time he'd checked. Ground Control tracked their attitude in detail, but with the velocities they would be traveling at during their mission, Jacob wanted to be sure they stayed on top of any necessary course corrections.

"Oh," he said aloud, as a thought struck him.

"What?" Derek asked. His tone was a little more terse than normal, but Jacob was too caught up in his own concerns to notice.

"Maybe we had a mag alignment issue after all. I think we're a little off-course."

"Really?" Vicky looked out her window, her anxiety ticking up another notch. She had no single constellation completely in view to reference, but she'd memorized the positions of the brightest stars she could see out her small pane.

"It looks fine to me," she said without thinking.

"That's because you're not a navigator," Jacob said absently. He'd spoken without heat or condescension, but with Vicky already tense, she bristled at the comment just the same.

"What do you see?" Derek inserted smoothly. He felt a slight twinge of unease at how often Jacob and Vicky had been getting under each other's skin since their engine tests had begun. It had all been minor and quickly resolved, usually without any intervention on his part, but these things could add up over time. Maybe he should have been more proactive in helping them find their feet as colleagues in the weeks before launch, but they'd been so busy with preparations and everyone had been rested and on their best behavior.

"I can't be sure," Jacob admitted, still focused on the stars, "but I think we're going to have to make a course correction, maybe soon. I'd like to ask about it."

Derek nodded approval and Jacob keyed his external mic.

"Ground, this is the *Pioneer*. Please confirm attitude, over."

Derek smiled at how diplomatic Jacob could be over the radio when he was so blunt in person. Instead of asking about a course correction outright, he'd just given a nudge to make sure Ground was noticing what he was seeing, leaving room to acknowledge that they might have seen it and just weren't ready for the crew to maneuver yet. But the silence that followed Jacob's radio call only served to remind Derek that they hadn't heard from Ground yet about the next step in their engine test. Another glance at the clock confirmed their next instructions were becoming long overdue.

"Colonel?" Vicky prompted quietly, unable to wait anymore.

"Yeah, I know. Ground, *Pioneer*, comm check. 1141 Zulu."

Jacob's head swiveled from Derek to Vicky and back again before he looked at the clock and realized what they were concerned about.

"Oh, wow," he said. "We should have heard from them by now."

"Switching to omni alpha," Derek said, flicking the necessary switches before engaging the mic again. "Ground, *Pioneer*, comm check omni alpha. 1142 Zulu."

They all sat in uneasy silence for several minutes while Derek debated what to do. Communications with Ground Control was their lifeline. Without that tether, they wouldn't know when to speed up or slow down, or how to make the precise course corrections to intercept Mars. They wouldn't be able to get into Mars orbit, or know how to fix any problems they might encounter along the way, let alone leave Mars orbit and get home. They couldn't even get home if they turned around right then; they needed Ground Control to guide them in to reentry. Without the ability to talk to Earth, their life expectancy plummeted; if *Apollo 13* had been without link, the astronauts would never have survived.

"Should I shut down the IPS?" Vicky asked. She sat very still, waiting for him to make the call.

Derek could hear the concern in her voice. He sighed. "Jacob, how far off-course are we?"

"Not far. I'm not even a hundred percent. Could be my eyes playing tricks on me."

Derek nodded. "Then we'll sit tight. A few extra minutes at this acceleration isn't going to break the mission. Let's give them some time."

"Yes, sir," Vicky and Jacob murmured together.

Jacob picked at a piece of dry skin on his thumb, glancing at Orion every few seconds as if it could disappear from view at any time. Vicky caught herself staring at the clock. She realized that she was clenching her jaw and forced her muscles to relax. She rolled her shoulders and started looking through her IPS status screens again, just to have something to do.

On the far side of the capsule, Derek took a deep breath and prayed for their communications to be restored. They sat together in the heavy silence, waiting.

CHAPTER FIVE

Jeff rubbed his forehead, wondering why all the problems had to occur during his shift. He looked at the two young airmen working Link. He knew he was glaring as he stood there with his hands on his hips, but he couldn't help it. As he watched, one of the airmen hung up the phone and fumbled with the push-to-talk button on his headset.

"Flight, Link."

"Go Link."

"Sir, we have definite confirmation on that solar flare being our culprit," the airman said, speaking rapidly. "Looks like it knocked out a few of our satellites before they could get the systems protected—it was pretty massive. The satellites have been rebooted, but there were some errors in the system resets and that's why we've been cut off for so long. They've finished trouble shooting and are doing another system reboot. If that doesn't work, they'll shift our comms to a different cluster like you requested, but they want to avoid that if possible—we're not the only ones who are being affected and they want to maintain essential systems for missile defense, et cetera. We should know if the reboot worked in just a few more minutes."

"Understood," Jeff said, almost surprised that he'd managed to follow the airman's rushed speech. He made a note on his mission pad and sat down to wait.

"*Pioneer*, Ground, comm check. 1231 Zulu." Paul's voice was calm as he made another attempt to reach the *Pioneer*. They'd lost link and communications nearly an hour ago, sending the room into a temporary panic. Jeff was grateful for how quickly everyone had settled down to wait, albeit impatiently, once they realized the loss was likely due to the solar flare they got reports of around the time they stopped receiving data from the *Pioneer*. They hadn't been completely sure of the correlation at first because of the time delays, but now that they had confirmation and reason to expect a restoration of communications soon, the whole room seemed to breathe a sigh of relief. There was a brief pickup in chatter and even a little laughter before everyone got back to work checking their systems in preparation for link restoration. Jeff hoped that the crew, who wouldn't know the reason for the interruption in comms, was taking the situation as calmly as the team on Earth.

"Flight, IPS."

"Yeah, go ahead."

"Can we revisit that mag alignment reading?"

Jeff sighed. Just before they'd lost link, IPS had reported another dodgy reading, but the issue had quickly been shelved while they tried to reestablish link and figure out what was going on.

"Yeah. You said it was the same thing as before?"

"Yes, sir. Same magnet; negative point two percent."

Jeff adjusted his collar and wished, for the fifth time that day, that the Wing hadn't decided everyone had to wear their blues on Mondays.

"Alright," he said. "So what are you thinking, a false reading? Instrumentation? Is it really off, but it's not enough to hurt anything? Or are we going to have problems with this?"

The IPS airman hesitated for just a moment. "Well, sir, we can't say for sure. None of those first three possibilities is really a significant cause for concern, given that the reading is within our margin of error. The only way this is a problem is if the mag's not seated properly. If that's the case, it could get farther out of alignment, and that could cause problems."

"Isn't that why we did a realign procedure?"

"Yes sir, but given that this has come up again at the same percentage of engine efficiency, it is a possibility. It's just not likely."

"What is the likelihood? George?"

The civilian contractor assigned by the team at the Jet Propulsion Laboratory that designed the IPS took his cue. "Very low, Colonel. Even though the reset didn't change anything, I'd say there's less than a fifth of a percent probability the magnet isn't seated. And even if that were the case, we'd see a gradual uptick in the misalignment readings long before we'd need to respond to prevent mission endangerment."

Jeff nodded and made his decision. "Then we'll proceed. I want to take an extra fifteen minutes after each benchmark increase in engine efficiency, though, just to make sure we have time to catch any changes before increasing velocity. As long as the reading remains stable at each step, you don't need to report it anymore."

"Yes, sir," said the IPS airman, who immediately leaned

over to work with Navigation on adjusting the *Pioneer*'s schedule of upcoming tests. They'd had to make a lot of adjusted calculations because of the aborted test earlier that day, and now they would be making more to increase the time spent at each level of throttle. Jeff made a note that the reading would no longer otherwise impact the engine tests, and hoped that would be the end of it—there was only so much wiggle room on a journey to intercept Mars.

"Flight?" Paul's voice came over the radio.

"Go."

"Do you want me to say anything to the crew when we reestablish comms, now that this has come up twice?"

"No," Jeff said.

"What if they ask about it?"

Jeff sighed. "Deflect. I don't want them using brain power on this."

"Roger."

Jeff looked over at Paul. There had been a slight pause before he answered and when he did, something in his voice had sounded a bit off. Jeff noted that his posture was stiff and he was definitely not giving any opportunity for eye contact. He disagreed, Jeff realized. He debated walking over to Paul to privately ask why and decided against it. The crew didn't need to know about something that wasn't affecting the flight, and which they couldn't do anything about.

Static filled everyone's headsets and the room grew silent. Every head turned to look at Paul, except for the airmen working Link. They were hunched at their computers, eyes darting across the screens as they checked their readouts.

"… Zulu, over."

Paul pounced on his mic button. "*Pioneer*, Ground. We read your comm check. What's your status? Message sent at 1239 Zulu. Over."

Jeff turned to the Link station. "Link, report."

The airman held up his hand for a few seconds before breaking into a smile. "We have link."

The room erupted in cheers and applause. Jeff shared their elation but he shushed them immediately. He didn't want Paul's ability to hear the crew's next radio call compromised. They settled slowly, the resulting din still louder than usual with chatter as different stations conferred on their new readings and continued celebrating. Jeff stopped himself from getting after them again. They wouldn't receive a response from the crew for several minutes still, and he realized that this moment was important for everyone's morale in the wake of the previous hour's tension.

"I want status updates as soon as we hear from the crew," he said instead, giving everyone time to analyze the renewed data stream, and sat down. He took a sip from his coffee cup, but he couldn't relax. Not until they had verbal confirmation that the crew was all right. Jeff spent the next several minutes listening in on the chatter and drumming his fingers on the table. Finally, the call came.

"Ground, *Pioneer*. We read you five by five, omni alpha, break. Status is good. We maintained twenty percect engine engagement during the disruption in comms, all systems green. Permission to increase to twenty-five percent and conclude the test, over."

Jeff shook his head. That crew was unflappable. "IPS?"

"The mag misalignment reading is holding steady at negative point two percent. We're good to go."

"Nav?"

"Good to go, Flight. We'll have an adjusted timetable as soon as possible."

"Good. Crewcom, tell them to go ahead."

"Roger that," Paul drawled. "*Pioneer*, you have a go. Increase to twenty-five percent and hold for thirty minutes as . . . uh, correction. Hold for forty-five minutes," Paul said, remembering Jeff's desire for an extra fifteen minutes in each phase of testing. "Then you can shut down the IPS. Over."

"Increase to twenty-five percent, hold for forty-five minutes before shutdown," Derek read back a few minutes later. "Any word on what caused our disruption in comms? Over."

"Yeah, *Pioneer*, that was a severe solar flare. It knocked out some of our satellites and caused temporary damage. We do not anticipate any further problems, over."

"That's very good to hear."

Paul smiled at the understatement and swiveled happily in his chair. He stopped swiveling when Jacob's voice came over comms, interrupting Jeff just as he began requesting status updates.

"Ground, *Pioneer*. Can we get verification on our attitude?"

"Stand by one, *Pioneer*." Paul craned his neck to look over the top of his computer screen at the Nav station two rows ahead of him. The airmen were busy scribbling calculations on paper, checking them against the numbers on their screens. Paul strained to hear but he couldn't make out the few words they were exchanging. At one point, the female lieutenant working the position unplugged her mic to walk over to Ecom. They talked for a minute, and the lieutenant plugged her headset in at Ecom's station and keyed her mic.

"Flight, Nav."

"Go Nav."

"Sir, we are going to need to maneuver, but we're still within acceptable parameters for now. Ecom and I recommend waiting until completion of all IPS acceleration tests instead of making multiple adjustments, to conserve thruster fuel."

"Understood. Crewcom, let them know."

Paul held down his external mic button. "*Pioneer*, Ground. We want you to maintain attitude until we're through the acceleration testing phases. We'll get you maneuver procedures at that time. Over."

"Copy that," came Jacob's reply a few minutes later, and that was that.

The atmosphere in Ground Control finally returned to normal levels of noise and tension. Paul leaned back and swiveled lightly until they received confirmation from the crew that the engine test at twenty-five percent capacity had been concluded. He stayed occupied with relaying standard orders for system checks and other housekeeping issues until Liz came to relieve him at the shift change, the same time the crew of the *Pioneer* would be shifting into their twenty-four-hour mandatory rest period. They'd take turns manning the Command Capsule, completing light duties, and sleeping. Ground Control, meanwhile, would continue their twelve on, twelve off shifts; the next engine tests would take place during Liz's shift in twenty-four hours. It was a good system, Paul reflected as he donned his lightweight blues jacket, ensuring that no one Crewcom had all the stress of working during high activity periods, while the other was bored with routine activity every day. It would be even better when Major Thompson returned from emergency leave to give them a third member to alternate with, and they could have days off like the rest of Ground Control.

"How long were we without comms?" Liz asked from the seat Paul had just vacated.

"Almost an hour."

Liz shook her head. "How did Colonel Williams sound when they came back?"

"Relaxed."

Liz laughed. "Yeah, that sounds like him. Thanks, Paul. Anything else pressing?"

"No, it's all in the passdown. Mag numbers are steady, et cetera, et cetera." He yawned. "You need anything else from me?"

"No, I'm good. Go home. Sleep."

"That will not be a problem." Paul gave her a lopsided grin. "Have a good shift."

"Thanks." Liz took a sip of coffee from her travel mug and settled in mentally for the next twelve hours. She depressed the external comms button. "*Pioneer*, Ground, comm check."

She glanced at the time so she could track how long the delay was now, and opened Paul's passdown document to read up on the previous shift while listening with half an ear as Colonel Amanda Chau, this shift's spaceflight supervisor, prompted Link to begin the round-robin section check-ins they did at the beginning of each new shift. Liz read through the section Paul had written about the solar flare and their resulting loss of link and communications. Just reading about it made her palms sweat.

"Ground, *Pioneer*, five by five."

Liz smiled at Jacob's familiar, clipped radio voice. It was so contrary to his personality in any other context. She wondered briefly how he and the others had handled their hour of radio silence.

"Crewcom?"

Colonel Chau's prompt broke into her thoughts.

"Radio check successful," she answered. Colonel Chau would have heard the radio exchange between Liz and Jacob, but procedure demanded a formal check-in. That taken care of, Liz listened intently to the chatter that started up once the check-ins were complete, maintaining her situational awareness of the various departments' conversations so she wouldn't be completely in the dark if the crew called in with a question or the spaceflight supervisor asked her to relay something. That focus was part of what made even the standard shifts in Ground Control so draining. Add a serious problem like total loss of link and comms, and the stress levels could rise dramatically. No wonder Paul had looked so exhausted when she'd arrived. Liz hoped fervently that the solar flare would be the only major problem they would encounter—their one obligatory mission glitch.

CHAPTER SIX

"I feel kinda sick."

Derek took a long look at Jacob while the younger man maneuvered into his seat and strapped himself in, preparing for the final phase of their IPS testing. They'd gradually increased the intensity of their tests over the last couple days to seventy-five percent of the engine's capability, and Jacob had been struggling physically.

"What kind of sick?"

"A little nauseous," Jacob said, "and we haven't even started the next acceleration test yet."

"Any other new symptoms?"

"Loss of appetite, but that kind of goes with the territory. The good news is, we now have additional food stores should we break down and have to wait for a tow," Jacob said, making an effort to be his light-hearted self.

"Have you taken anything yet?"

"No. I did let the flight surgeon know during my shift in the capsule and he said I could take anti-nausea pills, but I wanted to wait as long as possible."

"Okay. Take one now and see if it helps," Derek ordered.

"Yes, sir."

The relief in Jacob's voice reminded Derek of the times

he'd ordered his Type-A son to stay home from school when he had the flu. The thought warmed him.

"Any idea what's wrong?" He asked.

"Working theory basically comes down to 'space sickness,'" Jacob said, using air quotes.

Derek nodded sagely and waited while Jacob pulled an anti-nausea pill out of the small first aid kit attached to the bottom of his console.

"How's your mouth?"

"One new cold sore," Jacob said, "but the first one's almost gone." He took the pill with a sip of water.

"Sorry I'm late." Vicky flew into the capsule and dove for her seat, her feet narrowly missing Jacob.

"Whoa."

"Sorry."

"We still have time," Derek pointed out, but he only got a vague murmur in reply. Vicky was attacking her checklist as if she'd arrived an hour late.

Derek and Jacob exchanged a glance, Jacob's brow raised and Derek's furrowed.

"Abrams?"

"Sir?"

"Is there a reason you're so . . . ?"

"I've been thinking about the mag realign," she said, not pausing as she ran through the pre-test checklist. "One possible reason is some kind of anomalous reading on the angles."

"That is possible," Derek hedged.

"Right," Vicky said. "Even probable. And I'm not making any assumptions," she added as though she'd read his mind. "I'm just evaluating the possibilities."

"What'd you come up with?" Jacob asked, his interest piqued. Vicky tended to keep her mouth shut until she'd thought a problem through. Her refusal to speculate drove him a little nuts, but he was also learning to pay attention when she did speak up.

"The Hawking Engine is very complex. If any element is even slightly off, it can start to affect the mission. Now, this engine has been tested before in the two unmanned flights and, obviously, in the laboratory before that. Everything has worked perfectly, but what's never happened between missions?"

The two men came up blank and Vicky looked up from her work long enough to see it in their faces.

"It's never been serviced."

"Oh," Jacob said, feeling stupid for not guessing where her line of thought was heading. "Isn't it designed for repeated use? It's expensive."

"It's very expensive," Vicky agreed, "and it's even more expensive to have it serviced. You'd have to bring it back to Earth, which is not even one of its capabilities, and then get it in a clean room and completely take it apart and clean it and inspect it and put it back together again."

"Cheaper and easier just to build a new one?"

"Exactly, but not cheap enough to produce a new one for every mission. In the meantime, there is no way to inspect the engine's interior beyond sensor readings, and we don't know how quickly this kind of use will degrade the equipment."

"So you think it's developed an issue from repeated use?" Derek asked.

"It *could* have," Vicky corrected. "It's not beyond the

realm of possibility to think that something got worn down enough for a magnet to slip a tiny bit out of its locked position—it wouldn't take much, honestly. This equipment is very delicate. Now, there are enough safety features in the design that a magnet shouldn't become completely undocked, but it doesn't have to—if it just becomes unseated even a fraction of a centimeter, that could make a big difference in the readings—and potentially in functionality."

"Okay, take a breath," Derek interrupted. "Does this speculation do anything for us?"

"Well, no. Not at present," Vicky admitted, pausing mid-checklist, "which is probably why they didn't give us any additional information—we can't get inside and take a look, so why bother us?"

"Then why are you spending your down time working a problem we can't do anything about?"

Vicky blushed a little. "This is cutting-edge technology," she said, "and it's in my field. I know we're here to do a specific job, and I certainly won't let this interfere with it, but this is important, too. They aren't giving us details because we are Air Force astronauts on a mission to Mars, but we're also running a number of experiments, and I think it's a mistake to exclude the Hawking Engine and its performance from that mindset. Especially when it may not be performing as anticipated. I think that I, as the mission specialist, would be remiss if I didn't spend a little time thinking about this."

Jacob waited quietly to see what would happen. Vicky had never pushed back at Derek about anything before. He was surprised, and a little uncomfortable, to find Derek looking at him instead of answering Vicky.

"What?" he asked, feeling more alarmed than the situation warranted.

"You're the navigator," Derek said. "If the IPS is off by enough to show up in the readings but not enough to trigger a Caution and Warning or cancel the mission, could it meaningfully affect our approach to Mars? You already said it could be skewing our attitude a little. What do you think?"

"Uh..." Jacob stared at Derek for a moment, his brain oddly empty. He started speaking and, to his intense gratitude, his ability to think returned and caught up with his mouth. "Well, I'm not sure. I mean, the IPS isn't really my—but yeah, a misaligned magnet could affect our velocity and attitude—but the effects of a misalignment small enough that it doesn't trigger a Caution and Warning would be minor. Vicky might have a point, though. I mean, the whole reason she's here is so we have someone to deal with the IPS and help run all the experiments, right? Yeah."

Derek's lips twitched at Jacob's unfiltered, stream-of-consciousness response, and the way he'd backed up his teammate. There was no actual animosity between Jacob and Vicky, but this was the first time Jacob had come to her defense on something instead of arguing with her about it. Vicky obviously noticed it too, because she flashed an appreciative smile at Jacob before meeting Derek's gaze with a little more determination, and a hint of triumph.

"Alright," he said mildly. "Just don't wear yourself out."

"No, sir," Vicky answered, her voice revealing her surprise at his easy concession. She cleared her throat and tried again. "I won't, sir. Thank you."

"Mmm."

Vicky and Jacob exchanged a warm glance and Vicky got back to work on her checklist. She gave herself a moment to bask in the feeling of justification before she refocused on the task at hand. Conducting the IPS tests had gone a long way in helping her feel like she belonged on the mission, but this conversation had made her feel more like part of the team. It was still a little awkward between them, at least on her end, but she finally felt she'd made some progress.

"*Pioneer*, Ground, prepare for IPS acceleration test, Phase Five. Over."

"Copy, Ground. Stand by."

Vicky smiled as she completed her checklist. "Ready, sir."

"Ground, we are ready for IPS test, awaiting your signal."

"Smooth," Jacob said, appreciating how Derek had anticipated Vicky's early readiness and subtly let Ground Control know about it. It reminded him of the sort of easy, confident team dynamic they'd developed with Major Thompson. Not wanting to be left out, Jacob settled in and brought up his navigational system readout. He, too, was ready for the test.

"*Pioneer*, Ground, you are go for IPS test on Mark Echo five. Continue through the routine to one hundred percent efficiency as planned," Liz said over the radio, verifying the day's goal and referring to their pre-arranged start-time by the E5 brevity code. They'd made the planned switch from command-triggered testing to prearranged times as the lag in their comms increased.

"Roger that. Stand by." Derek tightened his seat straps. "Everybody alright?"

"Ready," Vicky said.

"Feeling fine," Jacob said, in his own shorthand to Derek about his nausea.

"Alright. We have two minutes and . . . seventeen seconds to IPS engagement."

Vicky looked out her window at the white stars against the darkness of the space between them, and mentally reviewed the IPS testing procedure, even though she'd already performed it multiple times during the mission so far, not to mention countless times in simulations. It was the final day of testing before they settled in for a monotonous few weeks of coasting before reversing the particle flow in the Hawking Engine and slowing down to intercept Mars and establish orbit around the planet. Vicky was fighting her brain's natural inclination to start shifting gears and think ahead to the IPS reversal procedure and what she'd need to do to continue running the onboard experiments. She forced herself to finish reviewing the IPS procedure she'd be executing in a minute. She didn't want to miss a step because she wasn't properly focused on the here-and-now.

"Stand by for IPS engagement," Derek said as the clock ticked down to thirty seconds remaining.

"Standing by," Vicky answered reflexively, pulling her gaze from the window to her console, even as she noted that Derek's prompts no longer bothered her. Everything was ready; she just had to press the button.

"And standing by on navigation," Jacob said. He was eager to see how the IPS tests would further affect their trajectory. Ground Control hadn't confirmed that they were slightly off-course, but they hadn't denied it either—the data Jacob had was not detailed enough to make a call on causation if they were, but given what Vicky had just said about the magnets in the IPS, he wanted to pay extra attention.

"Engage IPS," Derek said, and Vicky pressed the button.

"IPS engaged."

They went through the checklist, increasing the power and pausing between increases for the amount of time required for Ground Control to analyze their downlink data and intervene if necessary. They made it to their previous benchmark, seventy-five percent, without incident.

"Increase to ninety percent in five, four, three, two, one, mark," Derek said.

Vicky acknowledged the order and made the increase, then they waited. When they hit their next mark after a brief "looking good" from Ground Control, they punched it up to one hundred percent.

Vicky focused on breathing. They'd reached their peak acceleration and were experiencing their highest G-forces since launch. Next to her, Jacob checked their trajectory and marveled at how fast they were going.

"We just made history!" he said. "Again! And again!"

Vicky nodded. They'd already been traveling significantly farther and faster than any astronaut ever had, and that speed was increasing with every second that passed.

"This is going to be a tough adjustment back to zero-G," Derek cautioned. "How's everybody feeling so far?"

"Great!" Jacob said, grinning like a child. The anti-nausea medicine he'd taken was still working its magic and he could finally enjoy the thrill of what they were doing.

Vicky was starting to get a headache and simply replied "fine," and the crew fell silent as they monitored their systems and waited. They'd continue accelerating at this rate for nearly an hour, shaving a considerable amount of time off their journey to the red planet, and Vicky was already looking forward to disengaging the IPS and getting back to weightlessness so she could finally shift gears and continue her other work; they weren't allowed to unstrap themselves and move around the ship during IPS flight.

"What in the..."

Jacob and Vicky both looked at Derek when he spoke. Jacob did an immediate double-take and Vicky pulled herself forward to try to see over his shoulder, but he had half-turned in his seat and was blocking her view.

"What's wrong?" She asked, running through the possibilities in her mind.

Jacob turned and looked past her, his eyes wide. "Oh, crap," he said. Vicky followed his gaze, looking back out her window like she had earlier, and promptly did her own double-take. Instead of a static field of white pinpricks of light against the dark fabric of space, the stars slipped through the blackness, careening by on unpredictable paths and vanishing beyond the frame of her window, only to be replaced by new lights that appeared and similarly slid through space before disappearing out of view themselves. Some of them seemed to zoom around the ship, passing closely enough to leave Vicky blinking at their brightness. It was like watching the motion function of the European Space Agency's Star Mapper on fast-forward.

"What on earth?" Vicky looked away, suddenly very dizzy.

"Sir?" Jacob asked, enough distress in his voice to ignite a small flame of fear in Vicky that the strange behavior of the stars hadn't. His console was lighting up with Caution and Warning alerts.

"Shut off the IPS," Derek said immediately.

Vicky moved through her dizziness, almost glad for the tunnel vision she was getting because it meant she couldn't see the windows in her peripheral. She reached for the shutdown checklist, but her brain finally caught up with what she'd seen and she aborted the movement, reaching instead for the console. She uncovered the analog emergency IPS shutdown button on her left side and pressed it firmly. The emergency shutdown screen popped up on her glass cockpit console and the crew's world shifted as they stopped accelerating instantly and returned to a zero-gravity environment.

"Oh. No..." Jacob frantically pulled a barf bag out from under his console. He barely got it open and to his face before he started to expel the contents of his stomach. Vicky closed her eyes and breathed through her mouth. She was already feeling more nauseous than she had after launch, the sudden shift in G-forces exacerbated by the dizziness she still felt from the bizarre view out her window. Jacob moaned and Vicky opened her eyes again. She noticed Derek popping something into his mouth and theorized that he was taking anti-nausea medication. She grabbed at her first aid kit and opened it with shaking hands to retrieve some of her own. Jacob vomited again and Vicky felt beads of sweat forming on her forehead and neck. The console tilted and she frantically took a double-dose in hopes of countering the sickening effects of the vertigo.

"Mendez," Derek said to get Jacob's attention. He held out two small tablets, which Jacob accepted and quickly put under his tongue to dissolve. He pressed the barf bag back to his face in case they didn't work right away.

The crew sat together for a moment, just breathing and trying not to be sick. Vicky chanced another glance out the window. To her intense relief, the stars had stabilized. As she took it in, the console stopped spinning and she realized she'd been experiencing vestibular symptoms, becoming dizzy and nauseous when what she'd seen out the window didn't line up with what her inner ear was telling her brain about their movement through space.

"Ground, *Pioneer*," Derek finally spoke, breaking into her thoughts. His voice was strained, telling Vicky how acute his own symptoms were. "We experienced an anomaly and have shut down the IPS. Repeat: We have shut down the IPS. Emergency shutdown, break. We had a visual anomaly out all windows. I'm not quite sure how to explain it. It was like the stars were whizzing around. We also have several Caution and Warnings on the nav system, break." He turned to Vicky, turning off the external mic for the break in comms. "How's the IPS?" He asked.

"Uh, stand by one," she said, her voice shakier than she would have liked. She scrolled through her screens.

"Standing by." Derek keyed the mic again. "We have a trajectory warning," he said, leaning over to see the console in front of Jacob, who was still clutching the barf bag, his eyes firmly closed. "We have a nav system master warning."

"IPS green," Vicky interjected.

"We have green IPS status post emergency shutdown. Oxygen levels are normal. Power levels normal. Correction: Battery levels dropping slowly. All other critical systems green, break. Mendez?"

"Yeah." Jacob opened his eyes and lowered the bag slightly. "Um, I've got Caution and Warning on the GPS, positional data and trajectory. We are no longer tracking Mars' orbit. Or the sun," he said in surprise. "I don't have a reading on Earth, either. What the heck happened to my system?"

Derek relayed the information to Ground Control and requested a readback when possible to make sure they had copied everything in the transmission. "Is everyone alright?"

"Getting there," Jacob said, troubleshooting the navigational computer.

"I'm alright," Vicky said. She looked back out the window to reassure herself that the stars were back to normal. She mentally traced lines between them, repeating an exercise she'd performed a few times during the dull hours manning the capsule alone after IPS tests, but she couldn't make sense of them. She shook herself and started running through her post-emergency shutdown checklist, hoping it would help her get her focus back.

On the opposite side of the capsule, Derek was checking on the batteries in more detail, and between them, Jacob felt another wave of nausea. He looked up from his console in the hopes of getting his equilibrium back. He stared out his overhead visual navigation window, which was positioned at an angle between the console and the space directly above his seat. Jacob frowned even as his stomach started to settle. He had a moment of total confusion in which his brain seemed to stop functioning, and then suddenly he processed what he was seeing and his stomach fluttered with an entirely different kind of nausea.

"Guys?"

"Yeah?" Derek responded absently, still trying to figure out why the battery levels were dropping.

"I think I know why I'm getting some of those warnings from the nav system."

Vicky paused mid-checklist and looked at him curiously. "Why?"

"I don't know how, but we may have gotten a little turned-around or something."

That pulled Derek's attention away from the batteries. "What do you mean?" he asked, leaning over and following Jacob's gaze out the center window.

"I can't find Orion," Jacob answered, more calmly than he felt. "And given what we all saw a minute ago . . . "

Vicky frowned and looked back out her window. Her heart sank as she immediately saw what her brain had been too confused to realize before: She couldn't draw her imaginary lines between the stars because the patterns weren't there—they were different stars.

"That's very off-course," Derek noted.

"And we're going extremely fast," Jacob added.

For a brief moment, Derek wasn't sure what to do. He looked at his teammates. Jacob stared up at the stars out his window but Vicky was looking at Derek, still but wide-eyed. The weight of her expectation for him to have an answer settled heavily on his shoulders and he responded automatically.

"Ground will give us a procedure to course-correct," he said, the confidence in his voice genuine. "In the meantime, let's keep checking systems and troubleshooting."

Vicky nodded her understanding. Derek was right.

Spaceflight was and always had been controlled from the ground; they weren't alone up there. Ground Control would have all the information they needed to get back on course for Mars intercept, and to tell them what the anomaly had been. All the crew had to do was stay calm and be ready to feed information to Ground Control when it was requested. Vicky turned back to her console and got back to work on her checklist. The task steadied her, and with Jacob calmly doing the same thing beside her, she felt a little foolish for her fleeting moment of fear. She ignored several quiet *pings* caused by tiny bits of meteorite striking the craft, forcing herself to focus on her job while they waited for Ground Control's response.

CHAPTER SEVEN

Ground Control was buzzing with activity. The Link station was troubleshooting the downlink and uplink to figure out why they'd suddenly stopped receiving data from the *Pioneer* and started getting error messages back from the system, and the spacecraft monitor had said she received some anomalous readings from the craft's stress sensors just as they had lost the link.

"Alright," Jeff said loudly over his mic, "now that we know there's a problem and it's affecting all of us, let's do status reports. I want the most up-to-date information you have from the *Pioneer*. Round Robin."

The room quieted down as controllers sat back down in the chairs many of them had vacated in their anxious rush to understand what was happening. They began giving their reports in order of criticalness, just as they'd been trained. When it was the spacecraft monitor's turn to update the flight supervisor, there was a lull.

"Spacemon?" Jeff prompted.

"Hey, Flight. Um... can you swing back to me? That last batch of data I got is really weird."

Jeff grimaced. "Weird" was not a good word in relation to experimental spaceflight. "Okay," he said. "IPS?"

"We got a Caution and Warning, but the data set cut off mid-stream when we lost link. All we know is there was an issue with mag nine."

Jeff looked sharply at the airman working the IPS station. "That's the same mag we were having trouble with before, isn't it?"

"Yes, it is."

"No other details?"

"Working on it—there's more data here than we've had time to look through. Probably the best we can do until we regain link is guess, though."

"Understood. I want hypothesis as soon as possible. GNC?"

They continued down the list. Most of the updates were the same: all systems normal at time of link loss. Which meant the problem most likely did lie, as they were hoping, with the link itself.

"*Pioneer*, this is Ground Control. Please respond," Liz said over the radio, having passed the time it should have taken to get a reply to the comm check she'd sent immediately after they lost link. It was possible that whatever had interrupted their link could interrupt their communications but the list of causes for such a joint malfunction was small, and given that there hadn't been another massive solar flare, none of them were good.

"Link?" Jeff prompted. "Anything yet?"

"Not yet, Flight. I'm not getting any of the normal errors—just a generic disconnection notice, so it might take some time to figure this out."

"Copy that. Spacemon? You ready for us?"

The spacecraft monitor, a young second lieutenant,

turned around at her position and met Jeff's gaze, her face drawn into a sober frown. "Sir, I received some very strange readings in the last few milliseconds before the link went out. Multiple sensors on the craft's exterior picked up a sudden increase of hull stress at the front of the spacecraft. It's a huge spike, sir."

"Flight, Tracking."

"Go ahead, Tracking," Jeff responded automatically to the urgency in the airman's tone.

"We do not have a read on the *Pioneer*, sir. At all."

Everyone froze in place and Jeff stood to better see the young man who'd spoken. He was seated two rows ahead of Jeff, to the right, and he was swiveled around in his chair so that they could make eye contact.

"What are you saying, Tracking?" Jeff asked.

"I'm saying they are not appearing on any of our tracking systems. None of our satellites are picking them up. NASA has confirmed."

Liz spoke into the momentary silence. "How is that possible? There is no stealth capability on the *Pioneer*."

The airman gestured his lack of explanation. "It's like they vanished," he said, and the effect on the room was immediate. Everyone started talking at once, speculating and trying find some hint of the spacecraft's status or whereabouts. A few people left their stations to consult with other controllers, and the public relations officer was already giving instructions to his section on how to manage the story. The chatter rose so dramatically, Jeff would've had trouble hearing anyone over his headset if they tried to talk to him. It was, for a brief moment, chaos.

"Okay, everyone, settle down," Jeff said over the din.

"Settle! I don't want anyone to miss a radio call because they can't hear it. Crewcom?"

"Nothing yet, Flight," Liz responded.

"Alright, keep trying. Send out a call every five minutes with a timestamp. I want to give them as many opportunities to hear us as possible without confusing them about whether their own comms are getting through to us. Copy?"

"Copy."

"Nobody talks to the press or mentions this to their friends, family or social media—you know the drill. If you're asked about any of this, refer them to Public Relations. PRO, I do not want any press releases or leaks. Nothing leaves this room without my personal approval, or the approval of the wing commander. Understood?"

"Understood," the PR officer acknowledged briskly.

"Alright. Disappearing spacecraft is not a scenario we're prepared for," Jeff said to the room at large. "Do what you need to do. If you have questions, ask them. If you need to contact someone outside the room, remember to verify clearance. IPS?"

"Go, Flight."

"We lost contact during testing, so I want you to talk to JPL and bring in as many local engineers and physicists involved in the Hawk-E project as you can. If you need to fly someone in from California, let me know and I'll get them approval. Find out if anything could have happened to the engine to cause this. Does anyone have any questions?"

"Flight?"

"Who is this?"

"Ecom, Flight."

"Go ahead, Ecom." Jeff shifted so that he could see the airman in charge of monitoring the spacecraft's consumables.

"What exactly has been caused? What are we supposed to tell whoever we bring in?"

"Good question." Jeff picked up his pen and tapped it a few times against his desk. The room grew nearly silent as everyone waited for his answer. Finally, he looked up and his gaze collided with Liz's. She raised her eyebrows at him in unhelpful sympathy.

"Stick to what we know," he said, breaking the eye contact. "The crew was conducting their final IPS acceleration test. After receiving just over a minute of data while the IPS was at one hundred percent efficiency, we lost our link." He consulted his notes. "There was a significant stress spike at the front of the ship just before we lost link, and we are unable to verify their position because they're not showing up on tracking. Clear?"

"Clear, sir," the Ecom airman said, and several others murmured their agreement.

"Okay. We don't know anything yet. So let's get to work, and stay professional."

Airmen, contractors and civilian employees on loan from NASA returned to their jobs with a renewed sense of calm, and Jeff sat down at his desk. He sighed and picked up the secure phone. He moved the left earpiece of his headset to just above his ear and cradled the phone under his chin while he dialed the squadron commander's direct line. It was time to notify leadership.

"*Pioneer*, Ground, comm check. 1345 Zulu." Liz made her radio check and started the timer on her computer for five minutes. She opened a text document and started typing up her passdown. By the looks of things, she would not have a lot to do in the near future, and she wanted to get the details down before she forgot anything—it was going to be a lot for Paul to take in when he relieved her, and she wanted to be able to give him as much relevant information as possible so he wouldn't have to dig through the space-flight supervisor's room-wide passdown just to know what was going on.

Not that anyone knew what was going on. A disappearing spaceship? It was beyond bizarre. Liz figured Tracking would be asking NASA and the 50th Space Wing to check their satellites, but the chances of both organizations' equipment malfunctioning at the same time were slim. On an inspiration, Liz opened the digital accountability roster, which contained the personal phone numbers and home addresses of everyone in the squadron, and high-lighted Kevin Thompson's entry. The major was finally back in Colorado, but still on leave for another four days. Liz checked on Jeff and saw that he was on the phone. She debated for a moment and then picked up the unclassified phone at her desk and dialed.

He answered on the third ring. "Major Thompson."

"Hey, it's Liz Fischer."

"Colonel? What can I do for you?" His voice reflected curiosity and, if Liz was reading his tone right, annoyance.

"I'm sorry to bother you on leave, but I think you should come over to the Annex," she said, using the unit's shorthand for Ground Control.

There was a pause before he responded with a crisp, "On my way."

Liz hung up, feeling good about her decision. She was confident that, as the original mission specialist on Derek's crew, he would want to know what was going on as soon as possible.

Across the room, Jeff hung up from his call with the squadron commander. He took a moment to focus on the room's radio chatter to double check that he hadn't missed anything. When he was sure he hadn't, he glanced over to their Australian liaison, who had her secure line to her ear but looked like she was waiting for a response from the person on the other end.

"Liaison, Flight."

"Go, Flight."

"Are they notifying our crew there?"

"Yes, sir. They're also checking their tracking."

"Good, thank you."

"Flight, IPS."

"Yeah, go ahead IPS."

"We'd like to bring all hands on deck for this. Can we recall Major Thompson?"

Liz looked up from her passdown to see what his reply would be.

Jeff thought about it for a moment. "Crewcom, is he back in town?"

"He is," Liz said.

Jeff sighed. Formally recalling the major from leave would trigger official emergency status for the mission. He knew that, as Spaceflight Director, the call was up to him and nobody else, no matter how much they outranked him, but it was a big step. It meant notifying the families and issuing a sanitized press release. They could, alternatively, call the major in to brief him and then send him back home. Jeff scuffed the tip of his sage green boot against the floor a couple times. IPS's request for all hands on deck was not a request to merely notify the accelerator physicist.

"Yeah," he decided. "Go ahead and recall him. Formally."

"I gave him a heads-up while you were on the phone," Liz interjected quickly.

Jeff nodded and turned his attention back to the IPS airman, who'd paused with the phone receiver in his hand at Liz's disclosure. "Give him a call and let him know it's a formal recall, IPS. Uniform of the day."

"Roger."

"PRO, I need to see a draft press release ASAP."

"Working on it."

Jeff approached Liz's station so they could talk off comms. "Colonel?"

"Flight?" Liz asked, purposely addressing him by his position instead of copying his use of rank. She wasn't sure how he felt about her calling Major Thompson without permission, and she wanted to give him the freedom to tell her if he thought she was out of bounds. He couldn't do that as easily as her subordinate in rank as he could as the spaceflight supervisor.

"That was a smart move all around," he said, addressing what she'd done and why she'd done it without asking first. "Don't call Brightman yet, though. I don't want to wake him up."

"Wouldn't dream of it," Liz replied. "I figured I'd give him a ring about an hour before his shift. Maybe get him here a little early. It's going to be a complicated passdown."

"Sounds good." Jeff gave her a friendly nod and went back to his desk.

Liz's computer timer went off and she keyed up her radio.

"*Pioneer*, Ground, comm check. 1350 Zulu." She reset the timer and tried to go back to writing her passdown, but she found herself distracted by the activity she could see at the Personal Relations station. She knew as well as Jeff did what a formal recall of Major Thompson meant. The mission wasn't a secret—at least, the fact that Space Command had sent three astronauts on a mission to Mars with a top-secret new propulsion system wasn't—but Wing had kept a very tight lid on the details, even the unclassified ones. It hadn't been hard; very few news outlets had bothered reporting actively on the launch, let alone the flight, and the last flurry of speculation about the Hawk-E had taken place right after the mission date was announced. But declaring a mission emergency and not being able to state definitively that the spacecraft was intact and on-course was going to bring a whirlwind of scrutiny. Liz hoped they were ready for it—and all their families, too, especially those of the Alpha Crew. She resolutely pulled her focus back to her passdown and the chatter in her headset. There was nothing she could do about the press, but she could do her job.

"Colonel, I'm striking out here," Jacob said.

"Are the sensors not working?"

"I'm not getting any error messages or Caution and Warnings," Jacob said. "They appear to be working, but I'm not getting a match between the stars outside and any of the star charts in the nav computer—there must be an issue somewhere. I'm gonna troubleshoot some more, see if I can isolate the problem."

"So we still don't know how far off-course we are?" Vicky asked.

"No. I have no information about our position, or our attitude."

Derek finished the last line item in his capsule diagnostic checklist. "Well, we're not in any immediate danger, but we're going to be in trouble sooner than I'd like with these power levels falling like they are. Our link is still offline, so for now we're limited to voice communications with Ground Control. Abrams, how long has it been since we sent Ground our initial report?"

Vicky checked her watch. "About fifty-two minutes."

They already knew that it had been too long since they'd heard from Ground Control, but hearing the number made the reality of it settle heavily in the small capsule. For a few seconds, nobody moved.

"Okay," Derek said, putting all the authority he had into his voice, "here's what we're going to do until we reestablish communications. All of our consumables look good except power, so the first thing I want to do is limit consumption. Abrams, I want you to shut down the habitat, Protocol Three. Button it up tight—I don't want any problems when we power it back up later. Jacob, you keep working on navigation. I'm going to see if there's anything I can do to shore up this leak without knowing what's causing it."

"Yes, Sir."

"Got it."

"Okay, go. Get on it."

Vicky unstrapped herself from her seat and made her way to the habitat. She pulled the power-down checklist away from the Velcro strip holding it to the wall under the module's console. She had to force herself not to rush through the steps; they couldn't afford any mistakes.

It was a sobering move, shutting down the habitat. They weren't scheduled to do so until they were ready to detach from it and return to Earth. The whole point of the module was to keep them alive for the duration of their long journey to and from Mars, but there were partial shut-down procedures to allow them some flexibility if they needed it, mostly as power-saving measures in case one of their solar panels took any damage. Protocol Three was the most comprehensive shut-down they could perform without severing the link between the Command Capsule and the oxygen, power, and water systems contained within the habitat. It was only supposed to be executed in case of emergency, and with no way to troubleshoot their power leak with Ground Control, this was an emergency: If they ran out of power, they'd be dead long before they reached their Mars rendezvous point—not that they were headed in that direction anymore.

A shiver ran up Vicky's spine and she realized that her hands were shaking a little. She paused for a moment, quickly evaluating her symptoms for signs of hypoxia, but the moment passed and she was fine. Their oxygen levels were fine. It was just nerves.

"This is not helping," she muttered to herself, and resolutely continued working her way through the checklist, step by painstaking step. The sooner she finished, the longer they would survive.

CHAPTER EIGHT

"Alright, Mendez, what do you have?"

Jacob shook his head. "Nothing definitive. All my system checks are running normal, but nothing's lining up and I can't pinpoint the issue. There could be a problem where the sensor data is fed into the computer, or the sensors themselves could be malfunctioning. I have no indicators of any issues, so there could also be an instrumentation error, but again, I have no way of knowing where. I can't even say for sure that the star charts haven't been corrupted somehow—I need link with Ground Control to confirm they're intact."

Derek looked to Vicky next. The three were back together in the Command Capsule for a conference.

"Protocol Three has been executed," Vicky reported. "No issues. I think we'll be able to restart most of the experiments once we're functional again, but our crystal growth experiment is non-salvageable. I also ran a check on the airlock, and everything looks fine. We should have no trouble rebooting it in isolation if we need it to be operational."

"Good." Derek gave her an approving look for her initiative.

"You think we're gonna have to spacewalk?" Jacob asked.

The airlock was how they would get in and out of the ship, and it was considered a critical secondary system—not essential for life, but essential for long-term spaceflight, should anything go wrong on the ship's exterior.

"I hope not," Vicky said, "but what if we have to replace a solar panel?"

"We probably won't," Derek said. "All solar panel diagnostics are coming up clean. They just aren't taking in as much energy as they should, like they're turned the wrong way."

"They're supposed to auto-rotate to face the sun," Jacob objected.

"Yes, and they are auto-rotating. Just not like they should be, apparently. The program looks good and I'm not seeing any mechanical failure errors, but there it is. "

"Let me start checking these star positions manually. If the panels aren't rotating properly, maybe I can figure out where we are and we can override the automatic system to point them at the sun, or even rotate the ship instead."

"That's a good idea, Mendez."

"What about Link and Comms?" Vicky asked.

Derek shrugged. "I can't find anything wrong with them, so it must be something on Ground Control's end. All we can do is keep listening. Hopefully they'll fix the problem soon."

"You think it could be another solar flare?"

"Of that magnitude?" Jacob shook his head. "Extremely unlikely."

"Yeah, I just wanted to ask."

"Abrams, let's power down the IPS until we get our power ratios stabilized."

Vicky hesitated. With the onboard experiments shut down, if she powered down the IPS there would be little for her to do. Jacob would figure out where they were, and Derek would keep an eye on the ship's systems and make any necessary maneuvers. Vicky, on the other hand, was a mission specialist whose assigned tasks could no longer be performed. The fact created a kernel of irrational fear, and she thought fast to salvage her position and find something useful to do.

"Abrams?"

"Colonel, I'd like to download the IPS data onto my laptop first," she said, trying to sound neither tentative nor pushy. "It would only take a few minutes. Then I can go through the data and confirm nothing was wrong."

Derek frowned thoughtfully. "Is there a reason you want to do this? Beyond simple confirmation?"

Vicky's heartrate ticked up slightly. She hated speculating, but it looked like it was the only way Derek would approve her request. She'd thought a lot about what had happened while she shut down the habitat, and she couldn't deny a certain gut feeling, which she had no way to test scientifically without that data, and there was no telling whether she'd have another chance to access it. She took the leap.

"I think what we're experiencing might be related to our IPS test. The stars going crazy, the ship getting so far off-course—running the IPS at a hundred percent is the only thing we were doing differently than before. And then there's the matter of the main mag realign."

Derek looked out his window, turning his face away from Vicky while he weighed his options. She had a point—a very good point. He had the safety of the crew to think of, above all other considerations, and anything that used up more battery power before they figured out how to stabilize their levels would threaten that safety. On the other hand, he couldn't deny that something very strange had happened, and without Ground Control to help them, their long-term survival might depend on them being able to figure out what was going on by themselves.

It was a risky choice—authorize the action and potentially contribute to them running out of power before they could solve the battery problem, or wait so long to solve the mystery of their overall status that it would be too late to get home once they did figure out what was happening. His instincts told him that they were more than just off-course, and when it came right down to it, he trusted his people. Vicky knew their situation and was extremely methodical. If she felt strongly enough about the IPS's probable role in whatever it was they were facing to ask him to sacrifice power for information, he thought he should probably give her the benefit of the doubt. He offered a silent prayer for their safety and looked away from the window to meet Vicky's wary eyes.

"Okay. See what you can find out."

"Really? Great! I'll grab my laptop."

Derek had to chuckle a little as she sped off as if worried he'd change his mind. He looked at Jacob to share the moment, but Jacob was so absorbed that he hadn't even registered the conversation. He worked with his mouth slightly open, brow furrowed in concentration, manually mapping the positions of the stars he could see with the onboard sextant in hopes that he'd recognize some patterns and be able to figure out their attitude.

Derek checked their battery levels again and frowned. He knew the sun was in one of their blind spots because they couldn't see it from the capsule and Vicky had made a quick check out the Habitat windows and their exterior camera feeds. Their solar panel readings indicated they were pointed behind the ship, into one of those blind spots, so why weren't they drawing enough power to support the Habitat module? He started sketching out some possible scenarios in his notebook, calculating angles and percentages by hand. A flurry of *pings* heralded a collision with micrometeorites and his concern ticked up a notch. They'd already encountered more debris since the anomaly than they had in the previous week of spaceflight combined, and there was no way for Ground to let them know if they needed to maneuver to avoid anything larger. The *pings* subsided and Derek went back to his diagrams. They were flying blind and there was nothing they could do about it, but they could try to fix their power problems, so he focused on what was within his control.

Paul Brightman stood as Liz approached for her shift. It had been almost eighteen hours since they had lost contact with the *Pioneer*. Ground Control was crowded with people not only because of the shift change, but because all of the extra personnel they'd called in to work the problem.

"Any news?" Liz asked as she arrived at the Crewcom desk.

"No contact, to tracking," Paul answered efficiently. "They've got a bunch of physicists at work in room 105, and the Charlie Crew mission specialist has been recalled from Australia."

"Really?"

"All hands on deck," Paul said, gathering up his things. "The rest of Charlie Crew's staying put for now, wrapping things up. They'll be home soon. Meanwhile, we are making radio calls every half hour now. Actually, I wanted to talk to you about that."

"Go ahead," Liz invited. She took her service coat off and placed it on a hanger hooked to the station behind them.

"Okay." Paul resisted the urge to sit on the edge of the desk. Instead, he twisted his headset mic away from his face. "Given the state of things—no sign of the ship, no link or comms, et cetera—I don't see how we're doing any good here. Anyone can send out a radio call every half-hour and listen for a response."

Liz kept her face carefully neutral. "What are you suggesting?"

"I'm suggesting we leave Crewcom to someone else and get in the simulator. You know that's our best shot of figuring out what happened. Even if the physicists come up with a theory, it'll have to be tested in simulation, and in the meantime, we can work with the programmers on creating new sims to try to replicate what we know."

"We'll only be working with partial information," Liz pointed out, more out of habit than because she disagreed.

"Yes, but that's always going to be true. All we have to do—all we can do—is figure out what might have caused this and rule out what couldn't have. We don't need precise yet, we just need a basic idea of the possibilities."

"And when we do figure out the precise, we'll be ready to work on possible solutions," Liz added.

Paul did a mental double-take. "Yes," he said. "Yes, exactly."

Liz looked over to where Jeff was receiving his verbal passdown as he came on shift. "Alright, I'll talk to Flight. Are you good to stay on shift a bit longer while I sort this out?"

"Yes, ma'am."

"Great." After a quick internal debate, Liz took her service coat off the hanger and put it back on, feeling formality would work in her favor for the request she was going to make. She redid the buttons and straightened it out, checking to make sure her tie tab hadn't gone askew in the process.

"Hair," Paul said, and at her nod, reached out to remove the offending article from her left shoulder. "Thank you, Colonel," he said.

"It's a good idea," Liz said. "Truthfully, I've been thinking about it myself. I'm going to request the Charlie Crew mission specialist join us when he gets in. As the original Alpha Crew member, Major Thompson really should be here on the floor working with IPS—and he can always take over Crewcom if the *Pioneer* checks in. But I think we should have a mission specialist in the simulator with us."

"Definitely," Paul agreed. She was absolutely right about Major Thompson belonging in Ground Control for this, but he couldn't deny also being pleased that he wouldn't be asked to join them. Major Thompson was a by-the-book career Air Force physicist with a decidedly formal manner. Paul preferred working with the more relaxed Charlie Crew physicist, James Archer, although he thought Liz was probably motivated by the fact that James was more of an out-of-the-box thinker, which they might need as they simulated alternative theories of what had happened to the *Pioneer*.

Liz left Paul at the Crewcom station and approached the spaceflight supervisors' desk at the top center of the room. She waited patiently until their handoff was complete and Jeff had his headset on. He waved her over before starting his check-in, seeing that not everyone had finished handing off to their replacements yet.

"Hey, Colonel, what is it?"

"Paul and I have a suggestion," she began, and told him their idea.

"That's a great plan," he said, "and you're not the only ones to come up with it. We've fielded two requests already for you guys to get in the simulators, and the only reason we didn't say yes was because we wanted to give the *Pioneer* time to fix whatever's going on with the link and comms on their end before letting you go. But it's been eighteen hours now. They're still not showing up on tracking, which is beyond bizarre. So give me a few hours to make the arrangements and you'll all be released from Ground Control duty. I'll dismiss you as soon as I can so you can coordinate with Simulations, and we'll have you guys officially start tomorrow morning. I'll have scheduling send Paul a text."

"Thank you," Liz said. "And James?"

Jeff hesitated. "I think I should offer it to Thompson first. If he wants to stay here, I'll assign James to you."

"Perfect," Liz said, choosing her battles. "Thank you, Jeff."

"No problem."

Jeff turned his attention back to the floor and, seeing the crowds thinning, began his check-in with each station as Liz made her way back to Crewcom. She gave Paul a discreet thumbs-up on her way and he smiled his understanding. He stood as she approached again and finished gathering his things.

"It's all yours," he said, stepping aside so she could sit and plug in her headset.

"Flight says he'll have scheduling text you. We start in the morning."

"Excellent." Paul grinned. "I'm going to swing by 105 and see how they're doing before I go home. Have a good day," he said, and left the floor.

Liz logged in and accessed the passdown to read a more detailed account of Paul's shift. She pushed aside her impatience to begin the simulations work right away now that it had been approved. The morning couldn't come soon enough.

CHAPTER NINE

Jacob frowned at his star measurements. They couldn't be right. There was nothing in the view from their solar system that matched the pattern he was seeing.

He stared at his notepad, very conscious of the presence of his crewmates on either side of him. Vicky was tapping the corner of her laptop, sifting through for the IPS data she'd downloaded before shutting off the entire Hawk-E system. Derek was keeping an eye on their battery levels, tracking their continued loss of power. They'd shut down everything they could in the Command Capsule without guidance from Ground Control and their levels were still dropping. When he wasn't watching the power gauge, he was working on a new shift schedule. None of them had gotten much sleep since they'd lost contact with Ground Control, but they'd started taking a few hours off in regular intervals once it had become clear that they would be on their own for the foreseeable future. Now they needed to start settling in for the long haul, although with their power levels continuing to drop, it was unclear just how long that would be. At the current rate of power loss, the craft would be dead in the water in just a few more days. Their own deaths would quickly follow.

It was a sobering prospect, but Jacob had taken comfort and even a little elation in knowing that they were doing what they had been trained for. They were solving problems as they arose and taking care of each other—in space. He knew Ground Control would be doing the same, and sooner or later, their efforts would converge and they'd be back in contact and back on track. Right now, though, he was growing more concerned by the minute.

"Be right back," Jacob murmured, and headed out of the Command Capsule. He pulled himself into the habitat and took a good hard look at the light. A worry he wasn't ready to define was niggling in the back of his mind and he regretted not making a thorough check after Vicky's initial, quick visual sweep out of the Habitat's small windows right after they got off-course. All the artificial lights were off in accordance with Protocol Three, so the module was dark, save for a little light coming in from the upper right. Jacob pushed off against the floor to get to the window and looked out. Just at the edge of his view, he could see a bright glow. He checked the window to make sure the protective screen was in place and angled his head to get as good a view as possible, smushing his face against the screen until a tiny bit of the light source came into view. Although he could only see the very edge of it, he could tell it was small—much smaller than the sun ought to look from their distance. It was also much too red.

Jacob pulled back from the window, holding himself in place with two of the small hand grips placed strategically around the Habitat. He shivered in the relative cold of the dark module, which was only receiving what heat drifted in from the Command Capsule, and stared unseeing at the reflection of light on the far wall, which he realized was more red-orange than he had noticed at first, matching the hue of its source. For a moment, he just breathed. When his conscious thought process caught up to his eyes, he immediately pushed himself away toward the instrument storage panel next to the laboratory.

Among other things, the crew was meant to be continuing tests with a hand-held sextant for potential use in manual navigation through deep space, and a brand new handheld spectrometer NASA had developed. They hadn't started the tests yet—NASA, who had requested both tests and paid the Air Force to carry the instruments and conduct the experiments, wanted everything tested while the crew was cruising at their top speed.

Jacob yanked open the cabinet containing the spectrometer and pulled it out of its package, bumping his head in the process. Resuming his spot at the window, he pointed the device at what he could see of the star. Jacob swore softly as he realized that the instrument needed to be turned on. When it was ready, he anchored himself and pointed it as near to the center of the star as he could get without the wall of the module getting in the way, and pressed the capture button, waiting until he heard a beep. Then he waited again while the device prepared to display the results on the small LCD screen.

"You'd think in this day and age it wouldn't take so long," he muttered to himself.

Finally, the results displayed. Jacob swore again and pressed the print button. Once again, it took longer than he wanted and he nearly ripped the ticker-tape in half trying to detach it. He took two more readings to be sure and found them all to be consistent within the acceptable margin of error for the handheld device. Jacob hastily located the spectrometer's Velcro strip and adhered it to the ceiling. Then he jetted toward the Command Capsule.

Inside the capsule, Vicky realized she'd need to recharge her laptop soon. Derek wouldn't be happy about that. She was about to say something when Jacob reappeared.

"Hey guys?"

Derek half-turned in his seat to see Jacob as he floated up to their position.

"What is it, Mendez?" he asked. "You figure out our attitude and position?"

"Not exactly," Jacob said.

At his tone, Vicky stopped her work to look at him. "What's wrong now?"

Jacob cleared his throat, holding himself steady with a hand grip on the ceiling. "I think we're in a distant orbit around a red dwarf star, or maybe even just passing by it. M category on the hand-held spectrometer," he said, handing the printouts to Derek.

Derek took them with a frown. Jacob hovered where he was, avoiding eye contact with Vicky, who was staring at him open-mouthed.

"That's impossible," she finally said.

"Yeah," Jacob agreed, but made no effort to change his initial announcement.

Vicky roused herself and shut down her laptop. There was no way she'd be working on the data until they figured this out, and saving her laptop battery meant saving the *Pioneer*'s battery.

"How sure are you about this?" Derek asked Jacob.

"You want to take a look?" he said in reply. "It looks nothing like the sun should look, especially given our last verifiable position and velocity."

"I believe you," Derek said, "but let me see it anyway."

"Okay."

The two of them headed to the Habitat, leaving Vicky alone in the Command Capsule. She unstrapped herself so she could move to Jacob's chair and see the battery and power usage readouts on Derek's screen. She scribbled down a quick note of the levels and returned to her seat, but she didn't strap herself in. She looked out her window instead, taking in the still-strange pattern of stars and trying to take in the implications of Jacob's announcement. It was overwhelming.

Vicky could hear the deeper voices of the guys as they discussed their situation from the Habitat, but she couldn't quite make out the words. She pushed herself out of the seating area with a sigh and made her way through the access tunnel to the Habitat.

She found them at the far end of the module, Jacob balancing himself with a foot hooked into the wall, and Derek holding himself in place with a hand grip. They shifted as she approached.

"Want a look?" Derek asked.

She didn't, but Vicky nodded anyway. She took his place by the window and looked out. The edge off the star was unmistakably not their sun. The color difference was so obvious, she wondered briefly why Jacob had even bothered with the spectrometer, and why none of them had checked before. They'd been so focused on the essential tasks, and so used to getting all the answers they needed from their sensors or Ground Control, none of them had thought to take a closer look for the sun out the windows.

"What do you think?" Derek asked quietly.

"That's not the sun," Vicky said dully.

"And it's not a planet," Jacob added.

"Right," Vicky agreed. "So it's . . . it's some other star. It's some other star?"

"It appears to be," Derek said carefully.

"But it can't be," Jacob said. "I mean, how could we be orbiting some other star? I'm pretty sure this ship is not capable of interstellar travel. I think they would have told us if it were."

"But here we are," Derek said.

"Yeah. Here we are."

Another cloud of dust particles pinged off the spacecraft.

"So what now?" Jacob asked.

Derek crossed his arms. "Does the nav data fit?"

"The nav data?"

"Does the data we have access to fit the idea that we're no longer in our solar system?"

"I mean, as far as not being able to match anything to a star chart or find our own sun and planets, yes. It does. Add in this random star and I'd say it's a pretty sure thing," Jacob said.

"The stars scrambled," Vicky said. "Remember? Would they look like that if we were traveling faster than light?"

"Not that we're capable of that," Jacob added with a smile to make sure she knew he wasn't disagreeing. Still, it was a point they couldn't escape.

"Alright," Derek said. "Let's not worry about the 'how' just yet. Let's talk implications. If we're no longer in the solar system, we didn't just lose link and comms with Ground Control because of some technical difficulty. And our orbit around this star—if we're even in orbit—isn't giving us the power we need to maintain functionality on the spacecraft."

"So we need to change our orbit," Vicky said.

"We'd have to guess and check," Derek warned. "Get what information we can from the sensors and move into increasingly tighter orbits until the power levels stop falling, then get even closer if we're able so we can reboot the Habitat, all without taking too much radiation. Once we're in a stable position, we can focus on how we got here and how we're going to get home."

"How do you want to shift orbits?" Jacob asked. "Throw the IPS in reverse?"

"I don't know about using the IPS until we know what happened. Recommendation?" he asked, looking to Vicky.

"I don't recommend it," she said without hesitation. She was sure now that the IPS had to have at least played a role in what happened, and they didn't want to make any more unexpected side trips.

"Thrusters, then?" Derek frowned, knowing as soon as he said it that wouldn't work.

"There's no way we have enough fuel, Colonel," Jacob said. "Or time. We're so far away—using the IPS is the only practical way to maneuver enough to offset our power needs."

Vicky rankled a little at the sudden use of rank. She tried to tell herself he wasn't doing it on purpose to sideline her, as the crew's only civilian, but she honestly wasn't sure. Derek looked at her with raised eyebrow.

"It's not a good idea," she said firmly.

Derek sighed. "Mendez, that star is far away, but it's not *that* far. Is it so weak that it can't offset our power consumption without us getting significantly closer? Are we sure a long thruster maneuver wouldn't be sufficient?"

Jacob opened his mouth to answer but closed it again without speaking. He looked toward the window, even though at his current angle he couldn't see the star.

"Yeah, that's weird," he finally said. "I don't see how it's possible that we're not drawing enough power, unless there's a problem with the solar panels or how they're positioned."

"The diagnostics are clean," Vicki reminded him.

Jacob shrugged. "What if there's a problem with instrumentation?"

"There's no evidence of that," Vicky argued, getting tired of Jacob's tendency to jump to conclusions.

"Oh, like there was no evidence of a problem with the IPS? Or that we'd skipped across the galaxy?" Jacob demanded as the tension between them rose palpably.

Derek had had enough. "Hey!"

Both astronaut's heads swiveled toward him. Jacob's face hardened into defiant lines but Vicky had the sense to look embarrassed at their brief tiff.

"Listen to me," Derek said in his command voice. "You two need to figure out how to work together, because if we really are outside the solar system, and all the evidence we now have says that we are, we are on our own out here. There's not going to be a restoration of link with Ground Control. Radio comms? You can forget about it. We are who knows how many light years away and there is no such thing as faster than light communication. We are the only backup we have. So I don't want to hear any more of this petty arguing. Understood?"

"Yes, sir," Vicky whispered miserably.

Even Jacob looked contrite by the end of Derek's speech. "Yes, sir," he echoed.

Derek glared at them both for a few more seconds to drive the point home. He drew in a cleansing breath and let it relax his muscles so he could transition back to his normal demeanor.

"Now," he said more softly, "let's brainstorm the possibilities, no matter how far-fetched, and see which are best supported by evidence so we can decide on the best course of action."

The three floated together in silence as they all tried to come up with new ideas. Unsurprisingly, Jacob was the first to throw out an idea.

"So, if the star should be fully powering our solar panels," he said slowly, thinking it through while he spoke, "and there isn't anything wrong with them, maybe the problem is their positioning after all."

He stole a glance at Vicky, whose lips were pressed together as if to prevent herself from arguing. Derek was more encouraging.

"What do you mean?" he asked.

"Think about how the solar panels work," Jacob said more confidently, warming to his subject. "The system uses a steepest gradient ascent algorithm to automatically adjust the position of the solar panels to soak up the most sunlight. I can't believe I didn't think of this sooner."

"Oh," Vicky said in realization. "You're talking about . . . sir," she said eagerly, "the solar panels detect lumens, adjusting their position until they find the brightest point. When we left the solar system, they were angled toward the sun. With that no longer in the picture, they would have auto-adjusted, searching for a new light source."

"I see where you're going," Derek said. "What if they found one but it isn't our new star?"

"Exactly!" Jacob's eyes lit up with the possibility. "Maybe it's another star that's significantly farther away, or even a planet or planetary moon. The system would detect the lumens and, as the panels continued adjusting, it would detect when those lumens started to decrease as they angled away from the object. The system doesn't know there's a stronger light source out there so it stopped searching. It doesn't matter that it found a source too weak or too far away to keep us afloat—it found what it thinks is the best light source around."

"If that's the case," Vicky said, content to jump back in at the end of the speculation, "all we need to do is measure our angle to the star, override the system, and manually punch in the numbers to adjust the panels. Then we can turn the automatic system back on and the algorithm will keep the panels fixed on the star for the same reason it's kept them on the lesser source."

"And really, what else could it be?" Jacob added. "Nothing else we've thought of fits the evidence."

Vicky narrowed her eyes at the subtle dig, but Jacob was smirking at her and she realized he was teasing. Derek smiled at them.

"Nice work. *Both* of you," he said pointedly.

Jacob punched Vicky lightly in the shoulder and she tried to glower at him while she reached her hand out the steady herself against the side of the module.

"It's still just a theory," she reminded them.

Jacob crossed his arms. "At least it's something we can test."

"And we should do it sooner than later," Derek said, "in case it's wrong."

"Let me grab the handheld sextant," Jacob said, making for the storage cabinet that held the device so he could measure their angle to the star.

Derek headed to the Command Capsule to pull up the solar panel system override checklist and review the procedure for manually inputting angle commands, and Vicky again found herself with nothing to do. She set her jaw and followed Derek back to the Command Capsule to continue analyzing the IPS data. She'd work on it until her battery died or until they were ready to test Jacob's theory, whichever came first.

CHAPTER TEN

Liz and Paul were standing outside the simulations building when James Archer pulled his SUV into the parking lot. He parked near the entrance and the two Air Force officers ambled toward the vehicle as he got out.

"Morning," he said, scrubbing a hand through his short red hair.

"Morning," Paul echoed.

"How's the jet lag?" Liz asked with a smile, holding out her hand.

"Worse coming back than it was going." James shook her hand and then Paul's. "I had to dodge a couple reporters at the airport yesterday, too. How are you both holding up?"

"Staying focused," Liz said briskly, knowing from the sympathy in his voice that he was asking how they were coping with their former teammate being missing. They couldn't afford to think in those terms. As if in confirmation of her thoughts, Paul's face fell at the question.

"Let's get inside," Liz said hastily, and took her access badge out of her ABU pocket to hold it in front of the small badge reader outside the door. The little light turned green and the three of them entered the building.

Bluebridge was a brand-new building and large enough to house every simulations environment the Wing needed, in addition to offices and conference rooms. It was a secure facility, requiring special access badges available to a limited number of personnel. Once inside, the crew pinned their badges to their shirts and stored their cell phones and pocket knives in small lockers in the entry. Then they proceeded past the metal detectors and security guard, and down the wide main hall toward Conference Room 108C, where they were to meet with various representatives of the simulations team, the astrophysics and IPS teams, NASA, and anyone else who needed to be there. When they walked into the room, there was only one other person already there—Dr. Eliana Nour, head of the astrophysics department. She stood when they entered.

They all exchanged "good mornings" and chose their seats. Paul immediately leaned forward with his hands clasped on the table.

"I know you probably want to wait for everyone to be here, but can you give us a preview?"

Dr. Nour smiled sympathetically. "My team has been analyzing the data we received from the *Pioneer* just before we lost link, comms and tracking. We've been comparing that data with several anomalous readings from satellites and telescopes around the solar system and here on Earth, and we have a few theories as to what might have happened. We've had some preliminary chats with the IPS team, so we'll be jointly presenting a variety of theories."

"What's your best guess?" Liz asked.

Dr. Nour made eye contact with her and, to Liz's surprise, gave her a straight answer with no hesitation. "We believe the *Pioneer* entered a black hole."

Her proclamation was met with a moment of stunned silence and Dr. Nour nodded.

"That's impossible," Paul said.

"It is the best explanation for the data we received."

"Yeah, except for one small problem," Paul retorted. "The last time I checked, and correct me if I'm wrong, but I'm pretty sure there are no black holes extant in this solar system."

Liz touched his elbow lightly and he pulled back from where he'd been leaning over the table toward Dr. Nour.

"Nevertheless, that is our best guess."

Paul shook his head, looking away.

"Major Brightman does have a point," Liz said calmly.

"True," Dr. Nour began, but was interrupted by the arrival of the IPS team representatives. James immediately stood to greet them and direct them to seats next to his.

"I'll explain everything in the briefing," Dr. Nour promised.

Liz nodded her agreement and turned to Paul.

"You okay?"

"You know what they're going to say?" he said quietly. "You can't just fly into a black hole. It would tear the ship apart."

"I know," Liz said firmly. If the astrophysicists were saying the *Pioneer* flew into a black hole, they thought the ship had been destroyed. They thought the crew was dead.

Paul crossed his arms and leaned back in his chair so he could stare at his boots.

Liz tried to make eye contact with James, but he was engrossed talking to the IPS team. They kept their voices down, so Liz couldn't make out what they were saying. She almost asked, but decided to let James be. As an accelerator physicist, he understood the Hawking Engine better than she did. So she waited quietly, periodically greeting people as they filtered in for the meeting. Her patience was rewarded when, after presenting a few preliminary theories, each of which had been ruled "extremely unlikely" or "ultimately not possible" by the astrophysicists, Dr. Nour finally came to the theory of the black hole.

"I know it sounds far-fetched," she said as several people murmured their surprise and doubt, "but the data does line up with what we know about the formation of black holes. The fact that we can no longer detect any sign of a black hole in the area, suggests that it was unable to achieve stability. Nonetheless, the *Pioneer*'s disappearance at precisely the moment and in precisely the place a black hole may have been forming, seems too specific to be a coincidence."

"What does that mean for the *Pioneer*?" the squadron commander, Colonel McCoy, asked.

"We can't say for sure," Dr. Nour answered carefully, "but it is probable that the ship was pulled apart by the gravitation forces of the Schwarzschild Radius, or disintegrated in the collapse of the black hole. We're still analyzing the surrounding space."

Liz decided it was time to speak up. "Is there a scenario in which the *Pioneer* and the crew could have survived?"

"I'll hand that question off to the IPS team."

Liz watched with interest as a tall, thin man she didn't recognize took Dr. Nour's place at the front of the room, his bald head reflecting the overhead lights.

"Good morning. I'm Richard Liu, Chief of Development of the Propulsion Solutions Research Department at the Jet Propulsion Laboratory." As he talked, he handed a stack of thin, stapled packets to another scientist, who began passing them out to the two dozen people situated at the conference table and sitting in chairs around the edges of the room. "Our team has also been analyzing the data and working with the astrophysics lab ever since contact was lost with the *Pioneer* spacecraft. We've been particularly interested in the reported magnet alignment issues, the spike in hull stress at the front of the craft, and anomalies suggesting the presence of a black hole found in the data at and around the time the spacecraft disappeared."

He advanced to the next slide on the presentation, which displayed a graph of measured hull stresses experienced by the *Pioneer*. Reactions were varied but immediate—audible gasps, whispers, and even some incredulous laughter broke the room's quiet atmosphere. Liz leaned forward, puzzled by what she was seeing. The graph indicated that hull stresses increased, gradually at first but then sharply, with a particularly strong growth in normal stress at the front of the craft before suddenly plunging to below typical levels, and then climbing back toward typical levels almost as suddenly until the record ended.

"This figure," Dr. Liu said, "illustrates how the stress spiked, fell, and then rose again just before the *Pioneer*'s disappearance. Judging from your reactions, I think most of you have realized this is a classic N-wave, normally seen only during sonic booms. We believe the stress record was caused by two factors: First, an increase in matter density in front of the craft. This would explain this first increase in normal stresses. Second, a condensing of that matter by the spacecraft as it accelerated. The effect is similar to crossing the sound barrier—the craft pushed against the matter and condensed it even as the amount of matter continued to increase, until it reached critical mass, forming a black hole."

Dr. Liu paused, but nobody spoke and he continued. "We believe the matter was the product of the Hawking Engine, and that it was misdirected toward the front of the craft as a result of one or more magnets coming out of alignment. Thus," he concluded, "the *Pioneer* itself created this black hole. The craft apparently crossed the Schwarzschild radius just as it formed, and that is why they disappeared. Additionally, the black hole might have evaporated as soon as the craft disappeared. Both of these scenarios are unfriendly toward the idea that the crew might have survived. There is a—"

"Is this actually possible?" Liz interrupted. "To create a black hole with so little mass, and to cross the Schwarzschild radius as it's forming?"

"Theoretically," James said. "There's been some new research out of Doctor Wokurek's lab at University College London, which fits this theory. Wokurek is looking at primordial black holes, which are much less massive than stellar black holes. He's been able to identify two PBHs in the last three years, one of which has been experimentally verified. On the theoretical side, they've had some really interesting findings, which actually support the notion that the *Pioneer* could have created its own low-mass black hole and crossed the Schwarzschild radius as it formed."

"What about time dilation?" Paul chimed in. "If a black hole was forming, shouldn't everything have slowed to a stop from our perspective? The *Pioneer* would still be sitting out there while we panic about the formation of a black hole in our solar system."

"This is all New Physics," James said. "Maybe we didn't experience time dilation because they were already within the Schwarzschild radius, or maybe it's because the Hawking Engine was creating the black hole and the effects were therefore preceding the cause."

"What do you mean, the effects were preceding the cause?" one of the astrophysicists objected. "That is, by definition, impossible."

"Maybe not," James retorted. "After all, what does the Hawking Engine do? In principle, it works by reversing cause and effect."

"In an abstract, conceptual way," Paul hedged.

"It fits the data," James pressed.

"Could that explain the ship's disappearance?" Colonel McCoy asked.

"This is pure speculation," the astrophysicist argued. "Even if the ship did create a black hole, it would have been spaghettified as it crossed the radius."

"Spaghettification is the result of time dilation forces," Dr. Nour countered. "Since we aren't experiencing dilation, that is actually not a likely outcome."

James leaned back in his chair, crooking his left arm over the back. "Could the IPS have created an Einstein-Rosen Bridge?"

The room was plunged into silence and everyone stared at James.

"A wormhole?" Dr. Nour finally said, incredulity obvious in her voice.

"If the craft crossed the Schwarzschild radius, couldn't it also have entered an E-R Bridge, which removed it from the space-time of our solar neighborhood?"

"Whoa," Paul said, holding up his hands as if in protest as he realized what James was suggesting. "You think the *Pioneer* went through a wormhole?"

"This goes back to that research I was talking about," James said, undaunted. "The same team that produced those studies also found indicators associated with E-R Bridge formation."

"Yes, exactly," Dr. Liu said. "I was going to say there is a third possibility, and this is it. Maybe the black hole created by the *Pioneer* formed a wormhole. Once the craft entered the wormhole, it could have collapsed and caused the ship to disappear. Now, remember, it is most likely that, whatever happened exactly, the *Pioneer* and its crew are gone. However, if there was an E-R Bridge, it is also possible, however unlikely, that they survived, and were displaced elsewhere in the fabric of space-time."

"Perhaps we could look for additional evidence of an E-R Bridge," Liz suggested, "besides the data from the *Pioneer*."

Dr. Nour nodded her agreement. "And in the meantime, my team will keep searching for the *Pioneer* within our solar system. We've put in requests for satellite repositioning to broaden our search."

"But they could be anywhere," Paul said.

"Can we build any models?" James asked. "Is there no way to predict where a wormhole might have sent them? Something that could narrow our search parameters?"

"My team has already begun working on this," Dr. Liu

said. "We plan to start thinking of it as a random walk, and try to characterize the problem statistically. But with so little information ... " Dr. Liu finished the sentence non-verbally with an exaggerated shrug.

"Right." James tapped the table a few times with his fingertips.

The room grew quiet as everyone contemplated the impossibility of the search. If the crew had survived, Liz realized, they would probably run out of life support long before they were ever located.

"It's still most likely that they were torn apart or disintegrated," Dr. Liu said into the silence. "Unfortunately, we have no way to verify that at this time."

"Yes, we do!" Paul's eyes were wide as he looked around the table. "We do!"

"What are you talking about?" Liz asked.

"The entangled particles experiment! In the Mars Supply Module."

Understanding dawned and Liz started to grin. "You are a genius."

"Of course!" James said, catching on. "If the experiment is still running, the computer manipulating the state of the particles is still intact."

"Which would mean the *Pioneer* didn't evaporate!" Liz finished.

"Or get spaghettified," the astrophysicist said, but his tone was much lighter than it had been earlier.

Colonel McCoy reached for the classified landline receiver and dialed. "I'm calling DARPA."

Philip Schneider entered the astrophysics lab. Smaller than a classroom, its main feature was a long table supporting a large laser that was used in the bulk of the classified research taking place there. Philip said hello to the other two PhD students in the room, who were analyzing data on two of the computer stations set up along one wall of the lab. There were three smaller side rooms off the main lab. Dr. Coldwell, their supervising professor, had an office in one room; the second was a workroom shared between the students, and the third housed DARPA's entangled particles experiment. It was a small room with no windows, the only furniture a cheap desk with a rickety rolling chair with a missing armrest. On the desk was a small, high-tech container full of entangled particles, hooked up to a desktop computer that received input from the container and tracked the status of its particles.

Philip checked the time and decided to go straight to the Entanglement Room, as they'd dubbed it. He sat at the desk and logged in to the computer. The ever-running entanglement program had a long list of log entries from its frequent measurement of the particles, the neat line of 0s indicating that the entanglement was holding steady. Philip smiled as he noted the experiment's status in the official DARPA log.

Philip was one of a handful of PhD students in the Massachusetts Institute of Technology's Research Laboratory of Electronics granted access to the fourth floor of Building 26, having signed all the required nondisclosure agreements that threatened steep fines and possible jail time if they told anyone anything about the research being done there. The students were working on a variety of classified experiments, but the details of the entangled particles were beyond their level of clearance. Speculation ran high about the passive experiment they weren't allowed to fiddle with or ask about.

Regardless of the experiment's aim, what had started out inherently exciting because the students knew it was classified and cutting edge, had quickly devolved into something much less engaging. "Babysitting," they'd eventually dubbed the work. All they had to do was check the log every six hours and send an official record to DARPA. As the days and weeks had passed, almost every log entry had indicated that the particles were still entangled.

With his assigned check concluded, Philip returned to the main lab to work with the laser. He was just putting his protective glasses on when the door opened and Professor Coldwell entered the lab. She took in the room's three occupants and zeroed immediately in on Philip.

"Philip. When's the last time the entangled particles experiment logged an entry indicating continued entanglement? Have you checked the log?"

Philip stared at her for a moment in confusion. She was distinctly out of breath.

"Um, I checked it about eight minutes ago," he said, with a glance at his watch. "Everything looked fine. Why?"

"Eight minutes ago? Really?" The surprise in her voice threw Philip even more off-kilter.

"Yeah."

"There haven't been any gaps in the log? No switches from zeros to ones?"

"No. Everything's going normally. What's going on, Doctor Coldwell?"

"Nothing." The professor marched past him into the Entanglement Room. Philip peered through the open doorway from where he stood and watched as she logged in and checked the log going back what looked like a couple days. Philip exchanged looks with the other two students, who had both paused their work to see what was happening. One of them gave Philip a questioning look and he shrugged.

When he turned his attention back to the Entanglement Room, Dr. Coldwell was already walking back through the doorway.

"Philip, can I commandeer you for the rest of the day?"

Philip's interest was piqued by the excitement Dr. Coldwell couldn't quite hide.

"Sure," he said. "I was just going to get more data for my project with Bethany, but that's not urgent. What do you need?"

"Oh, you can still work on your own projects," the professor clarified, "but I want you to set an alarm. I want you to check that log every single hour, and if anything changes—anything at all!—you call me immediately, understand?"

"Absolutely."

"Good. Don't forget—every hour!" And then she was gone, leaving Philip and the other students alone once more.

"What do you think that was about?"

"I don't know," Philip said, frowning. It didn't make sense to be so excited about an experiment functioning as planned. He shook himself and set his phone alarm to go off just before four o'clock. He realized Dr. Caldwell hadn't told him when he could stop checking on the log, so he figured if he hadn't heard from her by the time his fellow babysitter Bethany came in to check it at her assigned time of nine o'clock, he would pass the new responsibility on to her. In the meantime, he turned his attention back to his and Bethany's project and put the protective glasses on to work with the laser. Whatever was happening with the entangled particles was clearly above his clearance.

CHAPTER ELEVEN

Vicky, Jacob and Derek watched the battery gauge, crowding together to see the display in front of Derek's seat. Their power levels had plummeted as they adjusted the angle of the solar panels, then started climbing again once they were in place. Now Derek had turned the automated system back on and they were hoping the levels would continue to rise and they'd be able to power up the Habitat again for a better chance at long-term survival. As they watched, the needle climbed with surprising speed.

"Yes!" Jacob punched the air. "It's going even faster now!"

"Should I power up the habitat?" Vicky asked.

"Not yet," Derek said. "I'd like to get back up to full batteries all around before we start turning things back on."

"Looks like it won't take long," Jacob said.

"In the meantime," Derek said, looking at the younger man, "you are officially off shift. Go eat something and get some sleep. I don't want to see you in here for the next eight hours."

Jacob's stomach growled and he grinned sheepishly. "Yes, sir. I might even treat myself to a chocolate pudding." He gave a two-fingered salute and unstrapped himself from the seat. "See y'all later," he said as he left the capsule.

"Abrams, you'll be off next."

"Okay. In the meantime, I'm going plug in my laptop and dig back into the IPS data if that's alright."

"Sounds like a plan," Derek said.

The two lapsed into an almost comfortable silence and Vicky opened her laptop to continue going through the IPS data. There had been no Caution and Warning indicators in association with the IPS when they lost contact with Ground Control, so she was looking for small anomalies—enough to potentially give a clue as to what had happened, but not enough to trip the indicator lights. Her one hindrance was that she didn't have access to all the data Ground Control did, and there was simply no way to overcome their inability to communicate with Earth—any signal they sent out would take years, if not decades, to reach their home planet, making any attempt a moot point; they'd all be long-dead by then.

Vicky sighed. That line of thinking was not going to help her analyze the data she did have. She took a deep breath and settled in to work, focusing all her energy on it and blocking out everything else. She jumped when Derek tapped her arm.

"Sorry," he said mildly, and she immediately didn't believe him. "You were engrossed."

"What can I do for you, Colonel?"

"Our battery levels are back up to max," he said. Vicky looked first at the display he was pointing to and then at her watch. Three hours had flown by without her knowledge.

"Habitat?" she guessed.

"Let's repower to Protocol One and see how we fare," he said, indicating that she should turn everything back on except their onboard experiments. They'd been an important part of her job when they launched, but now that their mission was survival and returning home, they were the lowest priority aspect of the mission.

"Got it," Vicky said. "Protocol One."

She affixed her laptop to some Velcro on the ceiling above her chair and made her way through the tunnel to the habitat, shivering as she moved into the colder space of the powered-down module. A quick look around told her by his absence that Jacob must be in the bedroom space, trying to sleep in the cold. She grabbed the habitat checklist from its spot for the third time since they'd launched, and turned to the pages that contained step-by-step procedures to power the habitat back up to Protocol One after a Protocol Three had been in effect. Bit by bit, the habitat returned to life, lights turning on, the airlock re-initializing, and finally, the climate control re-engaging.

Vicky looked around at the now brightly lit habitat, her heart filling with gratitude and a renewed sense of hope. She covered her eyes with her right hand and quietly recited the Sh'ma, as she had a thousand times in her childhood. She hadn't said it in ages and it wasn't the right ritual moment, but it felt appropriate to offer a prayer of thanks. She made her inspection and then headed back to the Command Capsule to give Derek a quick report.

"Habitat's up and running," she said. "How are the power levels?"

"Holding steady," Derek said. He blew out a breath of air.

"Excellent." Vicky got into her seat and grabbed her laptop from where she'd attached it to the ceiling.

"I didn't ask: How's the data looking?"

"Nothing really useful yet," Vicky said. "I wish we could talk to Ground Control."

"Yeah, so do I. So what's not useful?"

"Just all this data. I only have access to so much of it— the rest goes straight to Ground Control. It doesn't display nicely like it does for them, either, but I've about finished going through the reports that give me the matter and anti-matter production levels. So far everything looks fine."

"So we can rule out a malfunction?"

"We can rule out a production malfunction," Vicky corrected. "So the basic particle accelerator aspect of the engine was functioning normally, but there could still be other issues."

"Like magnet alignment throwing off the directionality of the matter and anti-matter streams?"

"Yeah," Vicky said. "Like that, except the only data I get on mag alignment is when there's a Caution and Warning triggered, and there wasn't."

"Right."

"There's still a folder for it in here somewhere, but it'll be empty. Let me see."

"That's alright. I believe you," Derek said, but Vicky was already looking for the folder.

"Here we go. Caution and . . . " she stopped, frowning.

"Warning?

"Folder size: twenty-six point three megabytes."

Derek looked at her. "Is there default content?"

Vicky double-clicked the icon to open the folder.

"Caution and Warning reports. Three of them." She met Derek's gaze, too confused for a moment to speak. Then she closed her eyes. "Instrumentation," she said. Something had triggered a Caution and Warning on the IPS, but her panels hadn't alerted her.

"Time stamps?" Derek asked.

"Just before the stars went crazy," Vicky said, her throat starting to feel tight. Seconds, maybe minutes before they'd somehow left the solar system. Maybe the whole thing could have been prevented if her Caution and Warning light had come on, but because of a short circuit, or a coding error, they'd never been alerted to the danger. And now it was too late.

"Three different reports?" Derek prompted.

"Yeah. It looks like this first one," Vicky said, skimming over the text, "is about guess what? Magnet alignment. Main mag nine was way over the margin of error. It happened a few minutes after we went to a hundred percent. This second one is a notice of several other magnets coming out of alignment. Not as badly but still over the margin. And the third one," she said slowly, as she opened the final file. "This one is a notice that the matter stream was shifted to a significant degree."

"How much?"

"It doesn't tell me that," Vicky said, frustrated. "Just that it was off."

"The engine is supposed to shut itself down if it's off by too much," Derek observed.

"Either it wasn't bad enough to trigger the automatic shutdown or that failed, too."

"'Trust your equipment,' they said." Jacob's voice made Derek and Vicky both jump. "Sorry," he said, floating up to them from the tunnel.

Derek looked at his watch pointedly and Jacob waved an apology.

"I woke up," he said. "Couldn't get back to sleep."

"Hmm."

"I see the habitat's powered up," Jacob changed the subject, still floating behind their seats. "How are the batteries?"

"Holding steady at fully charged," Derek said.

"Great. Oh, I visually checked the gel tubes on my way here," Jacob said. "They look okay, as far as I can tell."

"Good."

"I can't believe we didn't get the warning," Vicky said, still absorbed in the reports.

Derek looked at her sympathetically. There was no way she could have known there was an instrumentation error, but he got the feeling that she was kicking herself for missing it anyway.

"Even if everything had worked like it should," he said, "that doesn't mean we would have had enough time to react and prevent this."

"It is experimental spaceflight," Jacob said in solidarity. "There are bound to be problems."

Vicky didn't say anything, just continued to frown even more deeply at the laptop. Derek and Jacob exchanged a look.

"Why don't you go back to bed?" Derek suggested in a tone that Jacob understood to be an order. "You still have a few hours before your next shift. And try to actually sleep? Don't want those cold sores getting worse."

Jacob stopped halfway to the tunnel. "It's only one cold sore now. One. And it's almost gone," he said, and made his exit.

Derek allowed himself a smile before returning to more sobering thoughts. Now more than ever, he wished Vicky had been on the team for more than a few weeks before they launched. He wasn't sure if she was quiet and frowning in simple concentration or if there was an element of self-blame for their situation. And if there was, what was the best way to snap her out of it? A direct comment? Distraction? Derek sighed and decided to let it go for now. He would keep an eye on her and if it seemed to be bothering her, then he would say something. Liz, he knew, would have dealt with it on the spot, but he wasn't as light-handed at direct confrontation as she was. Better to wait, he thought, than accidentally antagonize Vicky—that was the last thing she would need if she was already being hard on herself.

Decision made, Derek relaxed. On Earth, he would have had to roll his shoulders and neck, but in zero gravity, all the pressure was off his spine and it would take a lot to strain a muscle. He turned his thoughts to their long-term situation. They would need to figure out what had happened, or what may have happened, and come up with a course of action to get home. It was probably a good idea to try to figure out where they were, at least in relative terms. The star they were orbiting did not correlate with the closest known stars to Earth, which meant they didn't have enough life support to get home the long way, but it was a relatively dim star. It was unlikely, but for all they knew, they could be right around the corner from home, their new star blocked from Earth's view by some other object.

Derek picked up his small all-weather notebook and jotted down a note to have Jacob work on determining their position, and to keep Vicky occupied with figuring out what had happened. He'd need to maintain some overlap in each of their shifts; they would probably want to consult each other. It would be a good idea to have all three of them at work at the same time for a portion of each day, as well.

As Derek made his notes, Vicky finished looking through the Caution and Warning data and started writing up a summary. As Derek feared, she was frustrated with herself, but more for not looking immediately at the Caution and Warning folder than for some false idea that she could have prevented their situation. She'd assumed that because the system didn't report a Caution and Warning on the Hawking Engine, there hadn't been one. That had been a mistake. But she also knew Derek and Jacob were right—looking again at the time stamps of the reports compared to when they had noticed the stars moving, and not knowing how long they'd been doing that before the crew noticed, she could see they probably would not have had time to prevent their current situation; they likely would have been relocated in space before she had time to shut down the engine, even if they'd reacted immediately.

Still, the IPS was her responsibility. It was becoming increasingly probable, rather than just being a gut feeling, that the incident may have been caused by the experimental new engine. She therefore had the best chance out of the crew at figuring out what the engine's malfunction had done to remove them from the solar system. Vicky created a table to compare what little data the Caution and Warning reports had given her and started checking other data files for relevant information, working methodically, making mental and written notes about various possible correlations and likely outcomes as she worked. Vicky actually started to feel somewhat exhilarated by the presentation of a puzzle—a problem to be understood and articulated. All self-consciousness disappeared and she lost herself in the work.

It was almost five hours later when a theory began to emerge. It was a crazy idea, involving black holes and wormholes, and she was still working on it when Jacob returned to relieve her. She mumbled a good night and took her laptop with her to the Habitat Module.

Her eyes were dry from all the screen time. Vicky stowed the computer and grabbed a pouch of eradiated beef stew for dinner, adding hot water. She closed her eyes while she waited for the packet to heat up, and images of home, her parents, and her older brother immediately flooded her mind. The pain the images caused caught her off-guard. She opened her eyes before it could sink in and moved to retrieve her laptop. She could work while she ate.

Derek found her still hard at it when he came to check up on her an hour later.

"Abrams?"

"Hmmm," she murmured, absently enough that he didn't think she was actual aware of his presence.

"Vicky."

She looked up, blinking as her eyes adjusted to looking at something that wasn't half a foot away from her face. Derek pressed his lips together to avoid smiling at the effect. It was adorable, like his daughter before coffee. He teared up unexpectedly at the thought and hastily refocused on Vicky.

"We're still in long-term spaceflight," he said in what he hoped was a neutral tone. "We still need to eat, sleep, and exercise, and you're off shift."

Vicky ducked her head. She had already discovered that relaxing wasn't going to work for her. She couldn't afford to be hijacked by homesickness, given their situation. Just the thought of it made her heartrate pick up. She looked at her laptop in desperation, her gaze falling on the time and date display in the bottom-right-hand corner.

"I have time," she said, almost belligerent in her effort to make sure her voice didn't shake.

"This is a marathon," Derek countered, his voice firm. "Not a sprint. The work will still be there in six hours. We will all still be right here."

Vicky frowned unhappily and Derek stared right back at her. With effort, she squashed a desire to argue.

"Fine," she said, trying not to sound too graceless, and saved and closed her programs. "I'll work out."

"And then sleep," Derek ordered.

"Yes," Vicky said, a little more irritation coming across in her voice.

Derek held up a hand in a silent gesture of truce and Vicky took a deep breath. Derek was only doing his job. She gave a little nod in return and put the laptop away. She'd spend her designated time on the Advanced Resistive Exercise Device and then try to sleep for a few hours. But there was no reason she couldn't continue thinking about her theory while she worked out, and she could listen to music when she went to bed.

With that unilateral compromise in mind, Vicky dutifully got changed for her workout.

CHAPTER TWELVE

"Hey, Colonel?"

Derek looked up from his dinner. Jacob was floating upside down, half in the access tunnel and half in the habitat.

"Yeah?"

"Vicky and I think we might know what happened. How we got here. Maybe."

"That didn't sound very confident," Derek noted.

Jacob shrugged. "It's theoretical," he said. "But neither of us can explain it any other way."

"You keeping an eye on anything up there?"

"No."

"Let's have a team meeting, then," Derek said.

"Team meeting" was the phrase they used when they needed to sit around the little table in the habitat and talk a situation through. Jacob gave him an upside-down thumbs-up and disappeared back up the access tunnel. He reappeared a moment later, Vicky on his heels. They all settled in around the table and Derek waved at Jacob to proceed while he finished his meatloaf.

"We've talked it all through," Jacob began, "and we think we must have gone through a wormhole, probably artificially created by the Hawk-E."

Derek paused in the middle of scooping up sauce with his spork. He raised an eyebrow and looked at Vicky for confirmation.

"We have no proof," she said unhappily, "but it is the most logical explanation for what we experienced."

"And where we are. Or aren't."

"There have been some recent studies touching on black holes and wormholes that supports the theory," Vicky added. "James Archer, Major Thompson and I were discussing the research on it in our reading group a couple months ago."

"Alright," Derek said neutrally, the fact that Vicky was on board with the theory helping him suspend his initial disbelief. "Does that explain the phenomenon with the stars?"

"Yes, sir."

"You said artificial?"

Vicky nodded. "With the magnets out of alignment and shifting the matter stream, it's entirely possible that the Hawking Engine created a dense pocket of matter or anti-matter around the front of the ship. At the speeds we were going, we could have started to create a black hole with an E-R Bridge inside it."

"Ramifications?"

"If we did create a black hole," Jacob jumped in, "obviously that's not great news for the folks back home."

"But if the black hole was being created by us, once we were removed from its space-time, it would have ceased to exist," Vicky said. "Theoretically."

"You've talked through all the other possibilities?" Derek asked.

"Extensively," Jacob said expressively, causing Vicky to roll her eyes and Derek to smile.

"I see."

"I don't like jumping to conclusions," Vicky offered in self-defense.

"And you haven't. You've worked the problem. How sure are we?"

"Pretty sure," Jacob said.

"As impossible as it is," Vicky agreed reluctantly, "it's the only thing we can come up with that fits all the data. What little we have access to, anyway."

"Including what we experienced and the reality that we're no longer in the solar system," Jacob said quickly. "I mean, last time I checked, the Hawk-E wasn't capable of opening a hyper drive window or going into warp speed, and those are the only other reasonable explanations for how we got here, so . . . "

Derek couldn't keep himself from laughing a little at Jacob's categorization of a warp drive as a "reasonable" explanation. Even Vicky's mouth quirked on one side.

"Alright," Derek said, bringing everyone's focus back. "We'll call that a solid working theory. Ideas on getting home?"

"We can run the IPS again and hope for a reverse trip," Jacob said.

"With no guarantee it'll work at all, let alone be control-lable," Vicky hedged.

"We can figure out where we are and try to use this star's gravity to propel us back in the general direction of home," Jacob said.

"Which will take too long—we'll get home long after

we're dead, if we ever get there at all."

"Alternatively, we could break out the remaining chocolate pudding pouches and spend our final months in luxury in the cold, unfeeling embrace of a distant star."

This time Vicky smiled fully, shaking her head more for show than out of any real disapproval.

"Okay, okay," Derek said. "Let's take some time to consider our options. In the meantime, Mendez, I want you to focus all your energy on figuring out where we are, if you can."

"Yeah, I've been thinking about that. I might be able to use spectral information to see if I can identify specific stars and triangulate our location. It's a longshot, but probably our best bet."

"Good idea. Abrams, just in case we do need to use the IPS again, I want you to work out how to do that with the best chances of replicating what happened and not causing something much worse."

"Yes, sir."

"Alright. Get back to work and don't forget to sign off when your shifts are over," he warned, wanting to reiterate his expectation that they stick to their new schedules so they didn't overwork themselves.

"Roger, wilco!" Jacob said, throwing him a casual salute. "I'll be up in the Command Capsule."

"I'll see you in a bit," Vicky said, and waited for him to leave before speaking again. "Sir," she said hesitantly.

Derek nodded for her to continue.

"Without detailed data and instructions from Ground Control, using the IPS with misaligned and probably unseated magnets would be extremely dangerous."

"I know," Derek said. "But we may not have a choice."

"Okay. I just wanted to make sure it wasn't overlooked."

"Understood. Hey."

"Sir?"

"I know you're used to working in certainties. I just wanted to say that you're responding to this crazy mess very well."

Vicky warmed at the unexpected praise. She'd been feeling pretty useless since they'd shut down the IPS. "I haven't really contributed very much."

"You found the Caution and Warning reports and contributed to a working theory of how we got here. And you've put up with a hypothesis-happy Mendez. That's not nothing."

"Right." Vicky smiled. "Thank you, sir."

"Sure."

Vicky headed for the Command Capsule to finish the last couple hours of her shift and Derek turned back to his meal. They were going to have to try to replicate what had happened if they wanted to get back home—he couldn't see any way around it. But Vicky was right. Without stable magnets and precise calculations based on detailed information from Ground Control, not to mention a simulation-tested procedure, any attempt to do so would be extremely dangerous and have little chance of success. A hundred things could go wrong and prevent them from getting home, if they even survived the attempt. They'd have to figure out how to mitigate the risk.

Ping. Ping, ping. Ping.

Derek looked to the walls of the spacecraft. They'd flown through so many fields of small particles since the anomaly, he'd almost gotten used to it. Even in Earth orbit, they'd heard the occasional tell-tale noise, but there was always the risk that something would penetrate the layers between them and the deadly space around them.

Even if the particles didn't punch any tiny holes all the way through, they could still cause damage to the outer layers. That was one of the reasons they had an airlock and space suits for each crew member—to patch damage to the exterior of the hull. Derek didn't much like the idea of doing a spacewalk for repair work in unknown territory without support from Ground Control, but they seemed to be flying through a particularly dirty part of the universe. The spacecraft's systems would let them know if anything breached the protective layers of material surrounding them, but that was an event nobody wanted to deal with. Derek reflexively checked the front left pocket of his flight suit for the emergency repair patches he kept there, but the alarm never sounded and soon enough the pinging stopped again.

Derek breathed out and turned his thoughts back to the issue of IPS risk management, absently finishing off his now-cold meatloaf.

"Explorer, Ground. You are looking good. Increase IPS to twenty percent."

"Roger, twenty percent," Liz said. She looked over at James in the right seat of the Command Capsule simulator to watch him punch in the numbers.

"IPS at twenty percent," he confirmed.

"How does that magnet alignment look?" Liz asked.

"Holding," came the answer over the radio.

The simulations team had been working around the clock to mimic what they knew about the Hawking Engine's performance throughout the mission and create a realistic simulation. If they could successfully and consistently replicate what had happened, they could start thinking about solutions. They'd undertaken several test runs with the Bravo Crew and James already, and the simulations team believed they'd finally got the parameters right.

"Okay, Explorer. Increase IPS to twenty-five percent."

"Timeline's a little fast," Liz objected.

"We've artificially calculated for the time the *Pioneer* spent at each percentage," said the voice.

"You're sure it's accurate?"

"We're sure, ma'am."

"Colonel?" Paul prompted.

"I just want to make sure we don't make mistakes because of shortcuts."

"Explorer, did you execute our IPS increase to twenty-five percent?"

"Go ahead," Liz said to James and keyed up her mic. "Increasing now."

"Roger."

"To be fair," Paul said, "we'd have to spend multiple days on each iteration of the sim if we kept to the actual timeline."

"I know," Liz said. "I just want to make sure we don't get careless."

"I hear that," Paul said, offering a smile.

Liz smiled back. "Doing okay, James?"

"Yep."

"Okay."

"Alright, Explorer, increase IPS to forty percent."

"Increasing, forty percent."

And so they continued, working their way up to ninety percent without incident.

"And one hundred percent on the IPS, please."

"Roger, one hundred percent. James?"

"One hundred percent," he repeated, and plugged in the command. The tension in the simulator rose immediately. James had to remind himself to blink as he stared at his display for any sign the engine was not performing as designed, and Liz almost held her breath as five seconds turned into thirty, then a minute, then two.

James' station lit up with a Caution and Warning.

"Caution and Warning, IPS mag alignment."

Another light flashed as soon as James turned off the first.

"Multiple magnet alignment warnings," he said over Liz's relay to their simulated Ground Control. Another light popped up. "I have a matter stream directionality alert."

"Okay," Paul said, as his own system joined the fray. "I'm getting Caution and Warnings too."

"Shut down the IPS," Liz ordered, and James immediately went for the emergency shutdown button. "Paul?"

"Multiple Caution and Warnings on the Nav computer. I've got a nav data error; star chart compatibility error; unable to confirm position and attitude."

"IPS shutdown complete."

The lights in the simulator came on.

"That's all we've got," the simulator tech said on the radio.

"Accurate?" Liz asked.

"Yes, ma'am. Everything lines up with what we saw from the *Pioneer*."

"Outstanding. Nice job, guys."

The crew took a moment to grin at each other, pleased they'd finally had a successful repetition of what had happened to the *Pioneer*.

"Now we just have to do it again to confirm," James said. "And again."

"Ground, permission to reset and run the sim again?"

"Granted, Colonel."

Liz took a few notes about the state of the simulated spacecraft. Detailed, accurate information was being recorded by the simulation program, but Liz liked to keep summary notes from one simulation to the next, especially when they were testing repeatability.

"I'm all set," James said.

"I'm almost done," Paul chimed in.

"Be thinking about your response times," Liz said. "We were expecting what happened, but they weren't. Give yourselves a few seconds of processing time when the problems start before you call anything out."

"Right," Paul nodded. "Guess we were a little too on-the-spot, huh?"

"The human brain can only react so quickly," Liz said with a smile. "You guys did great. Just slow yourselves down a tad when it all goes haywire."

"Roger that," James said.

"Okay, everybody ready?"

"Ready."

"All set."

"Ground, Explorer. We are ready for *Pioneer* IPS simulation, take two."

"Roger. Give us another minute. We're double-checking the figures."

"Copy that."

Liz relaxed in her seat.

"That really was a lot going on at once," James said. "Still. It's weird we never got a Caution and Warning report on the IPS."

"The system picked it up," Paul corrected.

"Exactly," James said. "So why didn't they report it? We got the verbal report of the nav warnings before we lost our comms, but those came up after the IPS warnings. Why didn't Colonel Williams report the IPS issues to Ground Control?"

"Maybe Vicky didn't report them to the Colonel in time," Paul mused, his voice tinged with doubt.

"There was a lot going on," Liz said, hesitant because she knew that wouldn't, or at least shouldn't, have prevented the verbal Caution and Warning report on the IPS.

"Well, we can ask them when they get back," Paul stated firmly.

"You're right," Liz said. "There's no use speculating. Vicky is a good mission specialist. She knew what to do."

"Yeah." James frowned at his screen. "I hope she was okay."

The other two looked at him.

"Well, the only reason I can come up with for why she wouldn't report the warnings is if she was somehow incapacitated."

"Vicky is fine," Liz said firmly. "If she wasn't, Colonel Williams would have reported it immediately. I know it's tempting to try to figure everything out, but let's take a page out of Vicky's book and not jump to conclusions. It won't do us any good. We don't know what happened in the capsule, and we won't know fully until we get them back."

James nodded unhappily. As two of the three accelerator physicists in the squadron, and the only two civilians on mission crews, James and Vicky had spent a good deal of time together training on the IPS and commiserating about the mindset adjustments they'd had to make to work with the military. He knew she was good at her job; she was better than he was. He just couldn't imagine her not doing her job properly and promptly unless something else had gone wrong.

Paul patted him on the arm. "She's fine," he said. "And if anything did happen, she's on a good crew. They'll take care of her."

"Yeah. I know. Thanks."

"Explorer, Ground. Prepare for simulation."

"Copy, Ground," Liz answered immediately. "Explorer standing by."

And they began again.

CHAPTER THIRTEEN

Jacob emerged from the access tunnel into the Command Capsule and rapped on a support strut.

"Knock, knock."

"Come on in," Derek said, looking over his shoulder as Jacob got situated in Vicky's seat. He took in the handheld spectrometer Jacob had brought with him.

"You don't like the onboard system?"

"It confuses the nav computer—it wants to match what I'm seeing to what it thinks I'm supposed to be seeing. I got tired of wrestling with it. The handheld's pretty accurate. Certainly accurate enough for my purposes."

"Think you can figure out where we are?"

Jacob shrugged as he peered through the spectrometer to aim at a star out Vicky's window. "Given how briefly we were in the wormhole, assuming that's what happened, I was thinking we probably aren't terribly far from Earth, relatively speaking. I've ruled out the closest stars—that was easy. But you know the majority of stars in our galaxy are red dwarfs. That's a lot to sift through. And they're not all in our nav computer because we're not supposed to be outside our solar system. What I really need is a direct line to Ground Control and access to a few super computers. Even so, it would take a while to figure out where we are. But if I can just find a spectral match between some of these stars and the charts on my laptop, there is a small chance I can triangulate our position."

"You don't sound confident."

Jacob lowered the spectrometer. "I've been making annotated local star charts, but we are the proverbial needle in the haystack—it's virtually impossible to know what field we're in from the inside of the stack. If that makes sense."

"Sure," Derek said with a raised eyebrow.

Jacob chuckled. "Yeah. I do have one theory, though, that I'm pretty confident about."

"Oh?"

"I was just thinking about this over breakfast. We could be inside a dark nebula."

Derek nodded his understanding. "All the dust storms?"

"Yeah. That and the relative scarcity of visible stars—plus a lot of them appear to be slightly red-hued. If we are in a nebula, red light waves are the most likely to make it through the dust."

"Mmm. Gel tubes still look good?" Derek asked. Vicky and Jacob were in charge of that experiment, so he wasn't sure when they'd checked on their radiation status last.

"Still looking good," Jacob assured him. "Vicky and I have been comparing notes to make sure we don't miss anything. The bubble count is slightly higher than what we were getting from our sun, but still well within our safe limits."

"Alright. Any other ideas on location? Besides a dark nebula?"

"I mean, we're talking about theoretical stuff here."

"Previously theoretical," Derek corrected. "Now empirical."

"But the theory isn't there yet," Jacob countered. "This is all New Physics, and these are not controlled experiments. We don't have the language or data to describe what's happened empirically. Anything I could say about our location is deductive guesswork."

"What's your best guess?"

"Assuming we went through a wormhole, its path likely followed a random fractal pattern, like a fracture on a bone. It's essentially Brownian Motion. There's no real way to predict what path it's going to take or where it'll end up. But since we weren't in the wormhole for long, it's a good guess that we didn't actually get very far from home. Relatively speaking."

"But far enough that we don't recognize where we are."

"Right. We're probably still in the Milky Way galaxy. We may even be in the same arm of the Milky Way. Even if we were only few light years from home, we wouldn't recognize the space around us because we're looking at it from such a different angle. As it is, if we are in a dark nebula, that gives us some idea of distance traveled—the closest known dark nebulae are five and six hundred lightyears from Earth."

Derek took a deep breath. It was one thing to know they'd gone beyond their solar system. It was another to put such a high number to their distance. Mars was only a fraction of a light-year away from Earth—its distance wasn't even measured in lightyears but light minutes—and it was still supposed to take them months using cutting edge propulsion technology to reach the red planet and return.

"So we definitely have to use the IPS to create another wormhole if we're going to get back," Derek concluded.

"Another wormhole could just as easily take us farther away."

Derek gave Jacob a scrutinizing look. "Getting pessimistic?"

"No, just . . . no."

Derek raised his brows at the younger man and Jacob gave up with a hint of a smile.

"I just don't think we're doing ourselves any favors if we don't have a healthy appreciation for the enormity of our problems. This whole situation is impossible. Any solutions will be, too."

"So we need to think outside the box," Derek encouraged.

"Yeah."

"Well, as long as we're on the same page. I'm going to leave you now," Derek said, noticing the time. "Oxygen levels and pressure look like they're holding steady, so I don't think we have any leaks, despite all the micrometeorite activity. Just keep an eye on it."

"Sir, before you go?"

"Yes?"

"Vicky and I were talking. Before we can use the IPS to go anywhere, she wants to try to check our theory and maybe get some predictions on the viability of recreating the wormhole and not ending up in the middle of a star or something when we do use it. She wants to build some models and run some simulations. Since you're the one with a computer science background, we'll need your help with the programming."

Derek nodded. "No problem."

Ping, ping, ping. Ping.

The two men made uneasy eye contact as the dust shower continued.

"I'm a little worried about all this space rain," Jacob said.

"Nothing we can do about it," Derek said firmly as another wave hit the spacecraft. Jacob turned back to his work with a frown.

Plunk.

The two men looked at each other again, waiting for any sign of a breach.

"That was a pretty good hit," Jacob said.

"You have your patch kit?"

"Yep." Jacob felt his pocket involuntarily. The kit was still there.

"Maybe we should pre-emptively divide and conquer," Derek said. "One person awake in the capsule and one in the habitat at all times. That way, if there is a breach . . . "

"We'll be able to get to it quickly no matter where it is," Jacob finished. "Good idea."

"I'll be in the habitat for the next few hours, anyway."

"Okay. I'll hang out here."

"Have fun. I'm going to do a quick visual to check for damage in the habitat," Derek said. "Just in case."

"Sir? One more thing, sorry. Um . . . Vicky and I were also brainstorming how we can make the best use of the supplies we have with us."

"You two talk about the Mars Storage Module?" Derek asked, anticipating the suggestion.

"Yeah," Jacob said, his surprise evident.

Derek shook his head. "I don't want to do any Extra-vehicular Activity just yet. We may have to eventually, but right now we're fine."

"Yeah, we'll need the water and oxygen and stuff down the road. But, uh, there's something else in the MSM we might want to grab sooner rather than later."

"Oh?"

"The entangled particles experiment."

Derek frowned. "That's a passive experiment for us, Mendez. It's meant to sit on Mars until NASA lands astronauts."

"Right. But in the meantime, it's being monitored on a regular basis by techs at MIT."

A few more pings sounded against the sides of the spacecraft. Derek sighed. "What's your point, Mendez?"

Jacob shifted to face Derek more fully, and Derek could see the eagerness in his face.

"If we can bring the experiment on board, we can use the interface to check on its status—the particles should still be entangled, and Vicky said the program keeps a log that will tell us if everything looks like it's supposed to— we just won't have confirmation because the link between our experiment's computer and the one at MIT would have been severed when we went into or came out of the wormhole, just like our telemetry and comms. But if the particles are still entangled and MIT is still keeping an eye on the experiment..."

"Then maybe if we fiddle with the particles, we can let them know we're still here."

"Exactly."

"We could also accidentally disentangle the particles."

Jacob shook his head. "Vicky said the entanglement is

very stable. They used a Bose-Einstein condensate."

"Hmm."

Vicky entered the capsule behind Derek. "Hey. I heard you two talking. What do you think, sir?"

"I think I need a more compelling reason than 'we could fiddle with it' to justify the risk of an EVA."

Vicky nodded in understanding. "We don't have any guarantees," she admitted, "but the experiment was designed for use on Mars. Some things might be planned later, but NASA would have pre-planned as much as possible; there should be specific procedures already in place for testing the limits of the entanglement and any possible communication applications. That would include initialization procedures, which should be outlined in a document on the computer for redundancy."

Derek shook his head in amazement at what his crew, and it seemed Vicky in particular, had come up with in a single brainstorming session. "So all we have to do is start the initialization protocol."

"Someone at MIT or NASA will recognize the pattern."

Jacob jumped in eagerly. "And the only way that pattern would occur, is if an astronaut on this end gave the computer instructions to take the necessary sequence of measurements to cause the particles to change state—or not change state—to create the code."

"It will be something obvious," Vicky added. "Even though they'd expect confirmation via the link between the computers, it will be an obvious pattern and they'll be able to deduce what's happening."

Derek looked between Vicky and Jacob. "You two are in agreement on this?"

"Totally," Jacob said without hesitation. "And we're both willing to accept the risk of an EVA."

"That's right," Vicky confirmed. "We don't know precisely when we lost link with Ground Control—it's quite possible they think we're dead. But if we can send a signal that only a live astronaut could send..."

"They'll know we're alive," Jacob jumped in. "They'll know they have to keep working the problem on their end."

"We don't want them to think they have to write us off," Vicky finished.

Derek sighed. There was as much of an emotional need to undertake this mission as there was a practical, scientific one, but he couldn't deny that the arguments were compelling.

"Alright. I'll consider it."

"Thank you, sir," Jacob said.

Vicky just smiled quietly.

"Abrams, have you gotten any sleep?"

"About three hours," she said. Sleep was hard to come by in microgravity at the best of times, even with sleeping pills. Under their current stress levels, three hours was pretty good.

"Alright. Let's talk about the MSM a little more, then. I want to review our knowledge and see if accessing the EPE is even possible—if it's not, this is all moot."

"Is that what we're officially calling the experiment now? The EPE?" Jacob asked. Nobody had bothered using an acronym for it before, since they had little reason to ever talk about it. Now that they'd be referring to it often, though, a brevity code made sense.

"Yes. EPE."

"Okay. Do we know where it is inside the MSM?"

"Hold on." Vicky turned around to go back through the access tunnel to the habitat and the men followed. They gathered around the table while Vicky headed toward her locker at the back of the module. She keyed in her pin and the door unlocked, allowing her to access her half-sheet notebook.

"You have personalized notes on the MSM contents?" Jacob asked, a little surprised, given that it was not a component of the ship they were supposed to have any contact with.

"Just basic structural info and a content diagram," Vicky said as she joined them at the table. She flipped through the book full of her personal mission notes until she found the fold-out page dedicated to the MSM.

"Here," she said, affixing the book to the center of the table and holding the page flat. "The exterior is pretty similar to the delivery capsule for a rover. We'll have to remove a panel and get around the parachute and balloon materials, plus the membrane separating all that from the MSM's contents themselves."

"Is this an accurate representation of the interior?" Derek asked.

Vick pondered her drawing, noting her placement of interior and exterior elements and trying to remember how detailed she'd made it.

"I think so," she said. "It's not schematic-level, but it should be pretty close to reality. I copied it from the official specs they gave us."

"We can work with this," Jacob said.

"I'll see if I have anything more detailed on my laptop,"

Derek said, thinking he remembered saving schematics and other technical data on every part of the ship, just in case. He excused himself to retrieve it.

"The EPE should be housed in compartment two, here," Vicky said when he returned. "If you can find anything, it would be nice to verify how these exterior panels line up with the interior compartments."

"Yeah, that's a good point," Jacob said while Derek searched his files. "That could make all the difference between opening panel Alpha, Bravo, or Charlie to access compartment two."

"Hopefully we won't have to remove more than one."

"Here we are," Derek said. He opened a folder marked *MSM Specs* and found a file that looked relevant. "Yes. This is what we need."

Vicky waited patiently for an answer to her query while Jacob continued scouring her hand-drawn diagram of the module.

"Ah, crud."

Jacob looked up at Derek's uncharacteristic statement. "What?"

"Problem number one." Derek turned the laptop to face the other two, and they crowded in to see what he was talking about.

Jacob groaned when he saw it; the official specs did not match Vicky's notes. She had the EPE housed in compartment two, but the official diagram showed it in compartment four. Vicky's face contorted into confusion as she looked from one to the other.

"I don't understand," she said. "I triple-checked everything in this notebook."

"I know you did," Derek murmured.

"So which one do we trust?" Jacob asked bluntly. "Vicky's drawing or the schematic?"

"Let me double-check this against the other info in here," Derek said, turning the computer back around.

Three small beeps interrupted them.

"Time to change the gel tubes," Jacob said, starting to move.

"I'll get them," Vicky said, and didn't wait for agreement.

Jacob raised his eyebrows at Derek. "Diplomatic," he said, sensing that she'd volunteered so he and Derek could confer quietly about what to do with the discrepancy without feeling like they had to be careful of what they said.

"What do you think?" Derek asked.

"Schematics don't lie," Jacob said.

"Vicky's very thorough," Derek countered, playing devil's advocate.

"Yeah, too thorough," Jacob said with humor. "But everyone makes mistakes."

Derek sighed. He studied her drawing again. It wasn't very detailed compared to the schematic, but what she had labeled was all there in the official drawings. The only difference was that the contents of compartments two and four were switched. What were the chances she'd gotten everything else right and that one thing wrong? Still, Jacob was right. However careful they were, human error was still the most likely source of problems in spaceflight.

"Alright," he decided. "We'll go with the official schematic."

Jacob gave a nod of approval and relief. Derek understood where he was coming from. He would be out on the spacewalk with Vicky, and being out there longer than necessary because of a mistake was not desirable—spacewalks were dangerous enough as it was.

"So if we decide to do this, how are we going to tackle it?" Jacob asked, shifting so they could both see the laptop screen as they began to discuss procedure. The MSM was not designed to be broken into during spaceflight, and that was reflected in the contents' relative inaccessibility. The schematic showed all the details of how everything was packed in there, and it wouldn't be easy getting through the protective layers to the EPE. They may not know for certain which compartment the EPE was in, but one thing was certain, no matter where it was stored: it was going to be hard to get it out.

CHAPTER FOURTEEN

In the end, Derek decided the potential benefits of retrieving the EPE were worth the risk of a spacewalk. They planned and rehearsed the EVA for two days, their preparations ending with Vicky and Jacob both sleeping and resting for eight hours so they would be fresh and ready to go—they couldn't afford any mistakes made due to sleep deprivation. Derek passed the time dozing in the Habitat Module and going over their planned procedures one last time.

Leaving the relative safety of the spacecraft was extremely dangerous, even under the best of circumstances with Ground Control watching through strategically placed cameras and providing guidance for the crew on how to proceed with carefully planned tasks. With no support and the crew making up their own procedures, it was even riskier. Given that, Derek wanted to make sure they were as prepared as possible

Derek had an EVA suit of his own on board, custom-made just like theirs. But Jacob and Vicky were the flight's designated spacewalkers and the mission to the Mars Storage Module was complicated enough to require both of them. Derek would remain in the Habitat Module, ready to provide whatever support he could as he oversaw the excursion.

Finally, the moment arrived. Three watch alarms went off at the same time and Vicky and Jacob emerged from their caves to eat; Vicky from the bedroom and Jacob from the Command Capsule where he'd been camped out. They ate quickly, keeping their eyes on their watches.

"Alright," Derek said when they were finished. "Are you two ready?"

"Yes, sir," Jacob said, as gravely as he ever had.

"Ready." Vicky nodded at their commander, not betraying any nerves.

"Let's get you suited up."

They moved to the aft of the Habitat Module. Jacob started pulling the components of Vicky's space suit out of its locker. Both of them were already dressed in the required undergarments. Jacob and Derek worked together to get Vicky into her suit, then Derek helped Jacob with his, Vicky assisting as she was able. Finally they were both in the main pieces of their suits, and Derek got them into their gloves, communication caps, and helmets. Derek took a proper nap in the bedroom while they floated in the module, pre-breathing oxygen from the habitat's supply for an hour.

It had only taken them a few hours to get dressed for the spacewalk thanks to all the practice they'd had on Earth, although Derek wasn't sure if zero gravity had made the task easier or harder. He was still tired when his alarm woke him from a light sleep.

"Mendez, Abrams, comm check," he said into the mic of his headset as he came out of the bedroom.

"I can hear you, sir," Vicky replied.

"So can I."

"Good. All set?"

"All set."

"Alright. Let's get you both in the airlock."

Derek unplugged them from the *Pioneer*'s oxygen, and so began the next part of the ballet. The airlock was small, barely large enough for Vicky and Jacob to both be in it at once with their tools. It took them a while, but they managed to squeeze in head-to-toe, attaching their safety lines to the hooks designed for that purpose. That way, if they lost their grip exiting the airlock, they wouldn't float out into space untethered.

Derek closed the hatch behind them and began the decompression process. The pressure in the airlock lowered to match that of the ship's exterior—the vacuum of space.

"Alright," Derek said when the lights turned green and the panel indicated that equilibrium had been reached. "You're depressurized."

Vicky reached out and opened the hatch with practiced movements. When they'd trained on Earth, they'd been under water, but it wasn't so different now—they'd been weighed down in the deep pool at the Johnson Space Center so that they were buoyancy neutral, neither rising naturally to the surface of the water, nor sinking to the bottom of the pool. Their suits had protected them in that hostile environment, and they had confidence in their equipment because of it. The hatch gave way and Vicky lifted it into place and pushed out against the layer of material covering the opening. Then she pulled herself carefully out of the airlock, grasping a handhold to the right of the doorway.

Finally, she was out, holding herself in place on the side of the ship. She clipped a second safety line to a rail and unclipped the first from the hook inside the airlock.

"I'm secure," she said as she moved out of the way so Jacob could make his own way out. Then she looked up. "Oh, wow."

They'd put the ship into rotisserie mode so that no one side was constantly in the heat of their new star, and the other in the devastatingly cold shadow cast by the ship itself. Spinning slowly on its axis allowed the spacecraft to absorb the heat evenly and prevented an overload of the heating and cooling systems. Since Vicky and Jacob were attached to the ship and more or less stationary, this technique provided an incredible rotating view of the space around them. Seeing it through the windows and the limited view they provided proved to be a very different experience from actually being in it themselves outside the ship. It was beyond expression, and Vicky found herself blinking back tears even while she grinned so broadly her cheeks had already started to hurt. She quickly lowered her helmet's sun shield as the star rose over the curved side of the ship.

"What?" Jacob asked. Vicky looked over and saw him emerging from the airlock, feet-first because of how he'd been wedged in.

"Wait until you get hooked in," she advised, marveling at the view while she waited.

The space around them was perfectly black, interrupted only by the red-tinged lights of distant stars and planets, and their new star when it was in view. It was significantly redder to the eye than the sun, giving Vicky just the otherworldly feeling she should have had in this situation. A disc, about the size of a dime, rose over the ship and Vicky's heart beat faster at the new discovery, presumably the cause of the solar panel confusion. The planet appeared mostly tan, but Vicky thought she could see some streaks of light blue. There were no visible rings, but the light reflecting off the planet produced a fuzzy glow around it. Vicky stared at it as it slowly arced overhead. Being stranded untold light-years from home couldn't dampen the thrill.

"Holy cow."

Vicky turned to see Jacob fully emerged from the airlock, looking out away from the ship. He laughed.

"How are things going out there?" Derek's voice came over their headsets.

"Fantastic!"

Vicky nodded. "It's quite the view, Colonel. Wish you could see it."

"So do I, Abrams."

Vicky looked over at Jacob. He gestured wordlessly at the space around them. He caught sight of the planet and pointed at it frantically.

"There it is! It's a planet!"

Vicky laughed. "I know!" she said. "It's amazing!"

"Alright, you two," Derek said over the radio. "We can talk about the planet later. Let's get this done. Make your way to the Mars Service Module."

The two spacewalkers maneuvered to the point where the habitat was docked with the Hawking Engine module, attaching and unattaching their lead lines to various closed-loop hooks on the side of the ship as they went. When they reached the docking point, Vicky tucked her foot into the farthest foothold there was and leaned out, stretching to reach the hook eye on the Hawking Engine. She secured her line and removed her foot from the Habitat Module, pulling herself to the next section of the ship. She made the crossing from one segment to the next without incident, and moved out of Jacob's way as quickly as she could. She immediately checked her gloves for damage and found none. Finally, she took a look at her pressure and temperature gauges and made sure that her tool tray was still secure before radioing to Derek in the ship.

"I've made it across." she said. "Equipment check positive."

"Roger that," Derek acknowledged.

Jacob made the transition and equipment check next, and they moved along the length of the engine. Not for the first time, Vicky marveled at the simplicity of the technology that allowed her to breathe and not simultaneously freeze and boil to death in such a deadly environment. It was a sobering, humbling thought.

"You realize we're in our own personal space ships, right?"

Vicky chuckled at Jacob's interruption of her thoughts. "Yep."

Derek's voice came over their headsets. "We're passing through another pocket of dust. Stay alert."

Vicky and Jacob both stopped moving. They kept their eyes on their space suits, watching as a few tiny bits of meteorite silently impacted their suits and bounced off. Derek gave them the all-clear when the impacts stopped, and after a buddy check, they got moving again.

They were a couple of minutes ahead of schedule when they reached the next transition, where they would leave the IPS module and secure themselves to the Mars Storage Module. This crossing was a little more difficult, with a wider gap between the two modules. Vicky had to push herself off the IPS to reach the MSM, but she did so without mishap. Jacob, two inches shorter than she was, had to do the same. There was a tense moment as he fumbled for a grip on the other side, even though he was attached to the ship by his lead lines, but he managed to grab the handhold and they were both safely across.

"Looks like we've arrived at panel Bravo," Vicky said, noting the tell-tale mark on the side of the module.

"Okay," Jacob said, pulling himself around. "Moving to panel Delta for our access point."

The two of them got into position and Jacob pulled out the power tool that would allow them to unscrew the panel.

"Ready?" he asked.

"Ready."

Jacob reviewed the procedure in his head and began his work, selecting the appropriate settings on the tool to do the job. There were twelve screws across the top and bottom of the panel, and thirty on each of the longer sides. As he removed each screw, Vicky secured them in a handheld magnetic trough so they wouldn't lose them. Finally, the panel could be removed. Jacob attached one end of a lead line to a small hook on the panel and the other to a hook on panel C. Then, using both hands, he pulled panel D off the side of the module. His feet grips kept him in place and Vicky took the panel from him and moved it out of his way, helping him straighten out so that he could grab a handhold again.

"Panel Delta has been removed," Jacob said, huffing a little with all the effort. "I'm going to take a quick breather."

"Roger that," Derek said.

"What can you see?" Vicky asked.

Jacob peered at the module's partially exposed interior. "A whole lot of stuff we're going to have to disturb to get to what's underneath it," he said. "I've got a lot of what looks like parachute material here."

"Alright," Derek said. "Then we'll proceed with parachute obstruction removal as planned."

"Right. Okay. I'm ready now."

Jacob and Vicky worked for more than an hour, moving the material out of the way and trying not to get tangled up in it. Finally, they reached the fabric separating the parachute from the contents of the module. Vicky handed Jacob the safety knife and he poised it over the material.

"Moment of truth," he said, and began cutting.

Vicky held her breath at first, hoping she'd been wrong and the EPE would appear under the fabric. Soon Jacob had a hole big enough to peer through. He turned on his bright helmet lights as they rotated out of the light of the star. He squinted.

"Okay, looks like a rounded surface," he said. "A hard surface. Definitely one of our storage containers. Let me make this hole a little bigger."

He went back to cutting through the divider material until he saw the edge of a symbol painted in white onto the container.

"Crap. It's an oxygen tank," he said as he cut farther to see the full O2 symbol. "Compartment four houses oxygen."

Vicky closed her eyes. She had been right; her diagram had oxygen in compartment four.

"Alright," Derek said calmly. "Let's get that panel reattached to protect the tank. Then we'll move to panel Bravo and check compartment two."

"Sorry, Vicky," Jacob said as he handed her the safety knife, his voice full of contrition. "I thought your drawing was wrong."

"So did I," she said honestly, tucking away the knife and moving to help him push the parachute material back into place so they could replace the panel. It was painstaking work but ninety minutes later the panel was back on.

"Let's try this again, shall we?" Jacob said, and they pulled themselves around to panel B. They repeated the same procedure when they got there, pausing once to weather another dust cloud.

"We should have music for this," Jacob said as he removed the panel. "I'm thinking Sibelius' second symphony."

"Sibelius? Why?"

"It gets very dramatic," he said as he started in on the exposed parachute material. "Sounds kind of like the soundtrack of a movie from the 1940s. Very cool."

Vicky smiled, helping him handle the mess of cords and fabric he was rapidly making. There was an increased sense of urgency since they'd wasted nearly three hours on the other side of the module.

"Is dramatic music really what we need right now?" she asked. "Wouldn't we be better off with something soothing?"

"Meh," Jacob said, pausing to catch his breath. "It would help us work faster."

"And stress us out," Vicky pointed out. "We might start making mistakes."

"Nah, we wouldn't make mistakes."

"You already did," Derek interrupted. "You decided to listen to music during an important spacewalk and it wasn't the soundtrack to *Star Wars*? Big mistake."

Jacob chuckled. "Excellent point, sir. Okay, Vicky, I think that's enough. Hand me the knife?"

Vicky obliged and Jacob started cutting. He paused for a moment when he got his first glimpse of the interior; another rounded canister. But he didn't know what the EPE container looked like compared to the others, so he kept going until he found a blue H2O.

"Okay, this is really weird and frustrating," he said, motioning to Vicky. "Take a look."

"What's wrong?" Derek asked.

Vicky saw the painted symbol and her heart sank. "It's water."

For a moment, nobody spoke. Then Derek's voice came back over their headsets.

"Water? It's the water tank?"

"Looks like the guys at NASA played a trick on us," Jacob said. "I mean, did they even pack the entangled particles? Was there some last-minute change we weren't told about? This is ridiculous."

"Well, you're not wrong," Derek conceded.

"So much for vindication," Vicky muttered.

"You get partial credit," Jacob said absently.

Vicky stared at the tank, thinking.

"So what should we do, Colonel?" Jacob asked. "Go panel-by-panel?"

"Let's cut more of this material out of the way," Vicky suggested. "Maybe we'll be able to see around the tank; get a glimpse of what's to its right and left. I think I can see part of the next tank over on the right. Maybe we can cut out some of the guesswork."

"It's probably a tank full of chocolate milk or something," Jacob said, but he started cutting again.

"Go ahead and see what you can see," Derek said.

Jacob cut the slit until it was the length of the compartment, then cut new slits from the center to the far right at the top and bottom. He pulled the long flap of material and held it out for Vicky to get as clear a view as possible.

"Mmmm, I think it's the nitrogen tank," she said, trying to angle her helmet lights so that she could see. "Yeah," she nodded. "I can just see the edge of a green-painted letter 'N'. It's nitrogen."

"Alright. Check the other side," Derek said.

Jacob handed the knife to Vicky and she cut the two shorter slits at the top and bottom of the compartment to the left. She held the flap back and Jacob took a turn peering in from his angle.

"I see another tank," he said. "But I can't tell what it is. No symbols visible from here."

He and Vicky looked at each other wordlessly for a moment.

"Sir? What do you think? Open up panel Alpha and hope the unknown tank is housing the experiment?"

"I think we're going to have to," Derek said. "Hold on, though. We're getting more impacts."

Vicky and Jacob immediately turned their attention to their own and each other's suits, watching the particle impacts and checking constantly for tears. A larger piece of meteorite ricocheted off Jacob's helmet and left a visible scratch.

"Whoa. You got dinged behind your visor," Vicky said.

Jacob checked his pressure and environmental readings.

"I'm okay," he said, right as the *Pioneer*'s high-pitched, intermittent tone came over their headsets, warning of a breach.

Both of them looked back down the length of the ship.

"There!" Vicky pointed.

"Yeah, I see it."

A tiny stream of white gas curled out of the Habitat Module. The ship was venting atmosphere.

CHAPTER FIFTEEN

Derek took a deep breath, knowing it might be the only one he'd get until the breach was patched. He ignored the shrieking alarm and the red emergency lights that flashed every two seconds, and scanned the habitat for signs of the breach.

The craft had Ultrasonic Leak Detector technology built into the framework—it couldn't pinpoint a leak precisely, but the inner skin of the craft was divided into segments with blue lights in the center that lit up when a leak was detected within twenty-four inches. It only took Derek a moment to find the blue light shining from a segment near the access tunnel. He torpedoed himself toward the spot, catching a handhold to arrest his motion so he wouldn't crash into the wall.

The hole was surprisingly obvious. Derek estimated it at nearly half an inch in irregular diameter—enough that the craft's life support wouldn't be able to maintain normal pressure. He was glad that they'd trained to breathe in air immediately in the event of a breach.

Derek removed a FastPatch from his pocket and peeled off the thin strip of paper from the adhesive side. He centered it over the hole and deftly applied the patch. The adhesive latched on to the white material of the spacecraft's interior and the last vestiges of suction finished the job. The patch was on.

The next course of action was to grab the nearest individual emergency oxygen kit. Derek pressed the mask to his face and flipped the lever on the small tank to start the flow of oxygen, just as the breach siren and the red warning lights desisted. He pulled the mask straps over his head and tightened them, reminding himself to breathe normally. Jacob's voice called to him over the radio, but he couldn't answer with the mask on. Derek pressed the small square of Velcro on the side of the tank to a Velcro strip on his flight suit so he wouldn't have to keep track of the tank. Then he moved to the habitat environmental monitoring station to check the pressure and oxygen levels. As he had suspected, the ship had lost life support too quickly for its systems to maintain normal levels, but they were already on their way back up. That, in conjunction with the lack of siren and lights, told him there were no other major breaches, but Derek wanted to be sure there wasn't any additional damage from the meteorite that had torn through the side of the craft. He searched around for any sign of the small rock and found it embedded in the material on the other side of the habitat—after it had punched through and crossed the habitat, it had carved through the innermost layers of the opposite wall, where it was finally stopped.

Satisfied that he was out of immediate danger, Derek returned to the airlock. A quick look out the window told him that Jacob and Vicky had crossed back over to the IPS module in case they needed to return to the ship. The environmental controls indicated that the habitat still wasn't back to normal EVA levels, so he left the oxygen mask on and pulled out the keyboard to type a message Jacob and Vicky would receive in Morse Code over their headsets.

OK, he typed. *Status Rpt?*

"We're fine," Jacob responded almost immediately, and Derek could hear the mingled relief and concern in his voice. "We could see the atmosphere venting but it seems to have stopped. Do you need us to return to the airlock?"

Neg. EVA, Derek typed. The *Pioneer* was recovering from the breach, and they needed to complete their Extra-vehicular Activity.

"Roger. Returning to the MSM."

Derek watched while Jacob and Vicky turned to head back to the MSM. He looked at his watch. He wasn't sure exactly when the breach had occurred, but by his estimate it only been three or four minutes. He shook his head. If anyone had asked him, he would have said it had been ten minutes, and he would have thought he was being conservative. He waited impatiently for the atmosphere to return to acceptable levels. When he was finally able to remove the mask and shut off the airflow from the tank, he stowed the kit and rubbed his face where the tight mask had made creases in his skin.

"EVA One, *Pioneer*, over."

"Hey! It's good to hear your voice, sir!"

"It's nice to be able to talk again. How are you making out?"

"We've just arrived back at the MSM."

"Alright, keep me posted."

"Will do."

Derek weighed applying a sturdier patch and working

on removing the meteorite from the wall against remaining by the airlock where he could best be of assistance to the spacewalkers should they need it, and quickly decided to stay put. The meteorite did not seem to have damaged anything other than the protective layers of skin around the spacecraft, since there had been no issues with electricity or any other detectable problems once he'd patched the hole; it could wait. Despite what had just happened, the two astronauts outside were still in the more dangerous position.

Out on the Mars Service Module, Jacob and Vicky were fitting panel B back into place. They replaced all the screws and moved over to panel A to start unscrewing it.

"I think we're getting faster at this," Jacob said.

"Just don't rush," Derek reminded them. "You still have plenty of oxygen left. No mistakes."

"Copy that."

Vicky took another screw from Jacob as they worked together to strip and remove the panel. Vicky saw the problem first.

"Oh, this is getting frustrating," she said.

"What now?" Derek asked.

"Stand by."

Vicky and Jacob, still holding the panel, stared at what it had been covering; a hard, white shell surrounded by more parachute materials.

"How old were those schematics?" Jacob asked.

"What's the problem?"

"I think we've uncovered the parachute dispersal mechanism," Vicky said. "We're going to have to detach it and remove it to get to the tank."

"Which may not even be the right tank," Jacob reminded them.

"Proceed with detachment and removal," Derek said, flipping through his notes from their pre-spacewalk planning. He was incredibly grateful he'd decided they should take the extra time to cover their bases and make sure they knew how to tackle any element of the module's interior that they might encounter. "You'll need to use preset five on the pistol grip tool."

"Roger that," Jacob said, changing the tool's torque and speed settings. He tackled the casing.

"Twelve screws," Vicky said quietly.

"Thanks." Jacob counted as he removed them and handed them off to Vicky. They were a different size than the panel screws, which she pushed to one side of the magnetic trough so they wouldn't get mixed up. Jacob gingerly removed the casing, exposing the dispersal mechanism.

"Casing removed," he reported.

"Alright," Derek coached. "We aren't going to be using this to send the module to the surface of Mars anymore, so don't worry about integrity. Just don't trigger the release."

"Right." Jacob examined the mechanism carefully, feeling gingerly around the sides to make sure it wasn't bolted down somehow. But the mechanism was seated securely in a plastic housing as the schematics had indicated. All he had to do was pull it out. Jacob tugged at the apparatus, but it didn't budge. He pulled with more and more force, bracing against the module with his knees for leverage. The housing popped loose suddenly and he let go, flailing his arms in a vain attempt to get his balance back.

"Whoa!"

Vicky reached out and grabbed his safety line. "Hold still," she instructed, and he quieted while she pulled him back toward the ship. "Okay?"

"Yep," he said a little breathlessly. "Never better. Did I break it?"

"Doesn't look like it," she said. "But we'll need to tug these lines loose so we can pull it away from the compartment."

"No problem," Jacob said, "but we should probably switch places now. I'm getting pretty fatigued."

"Okay," Vicky said, surprised he'd admitted it. She handed him the screw trough and he handed her the pistol grip tool, then they switched positions on the outside of the module. Vicky took on the task of clearing the mechanism from the module enough that they could get at the inner layer of protective material. She worked it farther and farther out, careful to avoid putting any pressure on the trigger mechanisms. The last thing they needed was an explosion and the faulty deployment of the parachute they'd already tampered with, especially since it would be happening right in their faces. But Vicky worked carefully and managed to expose the inner layer of protective material without incident. She cut through it with the safety knife.

"I can see the tank," she said, pulling the slit open as wide as she could with her hands. Vicky could barely make out the symbol of the entangled particles experiment—two gray strands entwined together with a white lightning bolt. She grinned.

"We got it!" she said.

"Wooot!" Jacob yelled so loudly that Vicky cringed.

"Excellent work!" Derek said. "How are you looking for removal?"

"I think we'll be okay," Vicky said. She cut the slit farther so that it ran from the top to the bottom of the compartment, then cut the shorter top and bottom slits to the right side before handing Jacob the knife to make the left-hand incisions. He held back his flap of the material and she pushed hers out of the way to reach inside.

"Can you get the bar out?" Jacob asked, referring to a curved plastic bar that the tank was attached to.

"Yep." Vicky retrieved the pistol grip tool from her belt. "Setting two, right?"

"That's affirm," Derek said.

She changed the setting and removed the two screws holding the bar securely on the frame of the module. Then she reached her hand around and removed the single screw holding the tank to the bar and gave screw and bar to Jacob.

"Attaching safety line," she said, and clipped a line to the top of the tank. She unclipped the other end from her suit and handed it to Jacob to attach to panel F.

"I'm going to unscrew the tank from the interior bar," she said, and reached in to do so. It was a tight fit with the pistol grip tool, and she couldn't quite get it angled properly to engage the screw. It just wasn't meant to be accessed.

"Having problems?" Derek asked.

"I think I'm going to have to detach the interior bar from the MSM's core so I can shift the whole thing around and get my angle," she said.

"Roger. Proceed."

"Do you need any help?" Jacob asked.

"Not yet." Vicky unscrewed the interior bar and pulled it away from the frame. "Okay, I think I got it." She rotated it to the right as far as she could and tried again to reach the screw connecting it to the tank. "Got it," she said triumphantly. The screw came out and she handed it to Jacob, but hesitated with her hand around the bar.

"Do we need to put the bars back?"

"I'd rather we didn't leave them floating around," Derek said after a pause.

"Roger. Screw?"

Jacob handed her the first screw, then the second, as she replaced the interior bar.

"So," she said, eyeballing the tank and the compartment opening. "Now we just have to get this out."

"Impacts," Derek said curtly.

Jacob and Vicky braced themselves for another round of meteorites.

"What are the chances there's another habitat breach?" Jacob asked.

Vicky frowned. "Slim, I hope."

"Very funny, Mendez," Derek said.

"Thank you, Colonel."

The shower passed and they got back to work.

"Three hours of oxygen remaining," Jacob murmured. Vicky set her jaw, tugging and angling the tank, sliding it out inch by inch. Just as it looked like she could pull it out the rest of the way, Vicky nearly lost her grip as something inside the module caught it.

"Mph."

"Whoa," Jacob said, grabbing the top of the tank. "You okay?"

"Problem?" Derek asked.

"Something's blocking the tank," Vicky said, examining the tank and the compartment visually. "I can't see it. Give me a minute." She reached in with her right arm to feel around the bottom of the tank. She couldn't feel any kind of detail with her thick gloves on, but she did find what felt like another bar just above the ring where the top and bottom sections of the tank were connected.

"Well, it's definitely the EPE," she said. "It has a center exterior connector ring. That seems to be what's stuck. I'm going to try to angle it away from whatever it's caught on. Stand by."

"You don't have much room," Jacob observed, but within a few seconds, Vicky had managed to guide the bottom of the tank out with her hand.

"Got it," Jacob said, pulling it the rest of the way out. He set it floating in space by the safety line and prepared to hand Vicky the outermost bar and its screws. When he looked back at her, her face was scrunched up in concentration. She was pressed against the module with her right arm still inside.

"Whatcha doin'? Looking for loose change?"

"My sleeve is caught on something."

Jacob regretted his levity immediately. He scooted closer and flipped his helmet lights on to see, but her spacesuit sleeve was covering whatever had it snagged.

"Let me help," he said, starting to reach in.

"No," Vicky said quickly. "You could get snagged too."

Jacob retracted his hand. "Colonel, are you copying all this?"

"I copy."

He turned his attention back to Vicky. "Just be careful," he said. "We don't need a compromised suit on top of a hull breach."

"Yeah," Vicky breathed, privately thinking that they may not get a say in the matter. Her arm seemed to be caught fast; she'd tugged pretty hard when she'd first tried to extricate herself from the compartment. She didn't say anything about it, though. Worrying the guys more wouldn't do any good. She checked the readouts on her suit and was relieved to find them normal. If her sleeve had been punctured, the object causing the tear must be plugging the leak. That small mercy would disappear once she freed herself, but it was possible the tear would be small enough that the layers of her suit or her arm itself could artificially seal the gap, or perhaps the suit's automatic pressurization system would be enough to make up for whatever life support was able to escape the suit through the tear. If it was a larger tear than the suit could manage, she would have to get back to the airlock—fast.

It comforted and calmed Vicky to review the scenarios in her head. She took a few more breaths and started to move her arm experimentally to try to get it loose.

"Careful," Jacob said again.

"Uh-huh."

Inside the Habitat Module, Derek listened silently to their quiet exchanges. He could hear the controlled anxiety in Jacob's voice and Vicky's calm concentration. He was grateful that trained astronauts were not prone to panic, although he himself was feeling the strain of waiting in the *Pioneer* with no ability to help. He kept himself off comms—no sense being a distraction—and simply floated with his arms crossed. All he could do was pray and wait for the outcome.

He looked out the window at his two crewmates, barely

in his field of view at the far end of the craft, still small in the distance.

"Come on, Vicky," he breathed to himself. "Come on."

CHAPTER SIXTEEN

Vicky concentrated on moving her arm this way and that, testing for give. She tried pushing her arm further into the compartment and then moving it away from the snag, but it didn't work. Anxiety finally started to build as a minute ticked by with no success.

"Just relax," Jacob advised, sensing her worry. "You'll get there."

Vicky nodded took a break, forcing her body to relax for a moment. She glanced down at her suit readings again and was relieved to find everything still normal. She resumed trying to free herself as another minute ticked by, and then another.

"This isn't working," she finally admitted. She shifted and reached in with her left hand.

"Whoa," Jacob protested. "You just stopped me from doing that in case I got snagged."

"I'm already stuck," she said, and focused on feeling for the snag. Working by feel was clumsy in the thick gloves of the spacesuit, but she finally found a hard protrusion between her right sleeve and the compartment's infrastructure. It seemed to have caught her sleeve just below the elbow.

"I think I got it." She slid her fingers along the unknown obstruction and grasped her sleeve, moving it around in place as gently as she could. It took her a while, but she finally managed to separate her sleeve from the object. Once she was unsnagged, she pulled her arms out carefully, and she and Jacob immediately examined her sleeves and gloves.

"Right there," Jacob said, pointing to what appeared to be a small tear in the outer layer of her suit where it had caught. "That could be a tear. It's hard to tell out here, though."

"Levels are still normal," Vicky noted. "I think I'm okay, Colonel."

"Not taking any chances," Derek said, as Vicky had suspected he would. "Follow protocol and get back to the airlock as fast as you can."

"On my way," she said, and handed Jacob the pistol grip tool without hesitation. She turned away from him and the open compartment and had to remind herself not to rush as she crossed to the IPS module, hooking and unhooking her safety lines. She made it back to the Habitat Module in record time, checking her suit frequently. Finally, she reached the airlock. She scooted inside and closed the exterior door behind her. Then she just had to wait while the compartment pressurized to match the interior of the Habitat Module. It felt like forever, but she was still breathing, and when the indicator light finally turned blue, Derek opened the interior door and pulled her in by her feet.

"You still good?" he asked, his nose involuntarily wrinkling at the incongruous smell of burnt meat she brought inside with her.

"Good."

Derek removed her helmet and gloves and Vicky pulled herself out of the way so that he could finish monitoring the spacewalk. She reached out and grabbed her gloves out of midair and examined them carefully, especially the left glove that she'd used to feel around for the snag. She found no problems, and stowed the gloves and her helmet. She then probed her right sleeve where it had been caught. There was definitely a tear, and longer than she'd thought—it was at least two millimeters, maybe three, and two layers deep. But the other dozen layers of protection had effectively sealed the tear and if any leaking had occurred, it had been counter-balanced by her suit's life support automatically increasing pressure to make up for any residual loss. Her preliminary suit examination complete, Vicky turned her attention back to the EVA still taking place.

Out on the MSM, Jacob had secured the outermost bar and replaced the parachute dispersal mechanism and its protective panel. Now he was working to replace the exterior panel.

"I hope Vicky's enjoying her time off," he teased as he wrestled it into place alone.

"She's eating your chocolate pudding," Derek deadpanned.

"What? Here I am, risking my life, and what's the thanks I get? Robbery. Robbery! Is there no respect for heroism anymore?"

Derek grinned and Vicky rolled her eyes. Without her help, it took Jacob longer than usual to finish replacing all the screws. When he was finally done, he hooked another safety line to the EPE and unhooked its first line from the side of the module, attaching it instead to his suit to create a double bond with the cylinder.

"Okay," he said. "I'm coming back."

"Glove check," Derek ordered.

"Looking good," Jacob replied a minute later. "Should I check the hull breach damage?"

"Yes, but don't linger," Derek instructed, knowing Jacob barely had an hour of oxygen left in his suit.

"Roger."

Jacob began his painstaking journey back to the airlock with the EPE floating along with him like a dog on a leash. Once he was back on the Habitat Module, Derek guided him to the location of the breach.

"It doesn't look bad," Jacob reported. "It's about half an inch in diameter, but it looks like a clean shot to the interior—no damage to additional structures or systems that I can see."

"That confirms what I suspected," Derek said. "Come on back."

"How much oxygen did we lose?" Vicky asked. She rotated her right wrist experimentally; it felt a little stiff. There wasn't much movement possible in the EVA suits, but she'd done a lot with her right arm and wrist trying to get free from the compartment.

"I don't know yet. We'll do a complete inventory and systems check once the EVA is over."

"Okay." On the one hand, Vicky knew that it didn't matter how much they'd lost. There was nothing they could do about it; they couldn't even abort the mission and make an early return to Earth. Any loss of life support was something they'd just have to deal with. On the other hand, information was their greatest ally. It could wait, but they wouldn't want to leave it very long.

"I've reached the airlock. Opening the exterior door."

Soon Jacob was pulling himself and the EPE tank into the airlock. They all waited for it to pressurize, and Vicky offered him a mock-critical look when she and Derek finally pulled him back into the Habitat Module.

"What took you so long?"

Jacob grinned in appreciation. "You're just jealous I hold the record for longest EVA this far from Earth." He patted the EPE. "We did it."

Derek relaxed in the middle of the habitat. "Yes, we did. Nice job, both of you. Vicky, you spent six hours four minutes and twelve seconds on EVA. Jacob, you did seven hours, fifty-eight minutes and forty-nine seconds."

"Can we round that up to eight hours?"

"No."

"Worth a try. Can I get out of this suit before it runs out of oxygen?"

"That we can do," Derek said.

"Did you barbeque something out there?" Vicky teased while she removed one of his gloves.

"Oh, does it really smell like charred meat?"

"Yeah, it definitely does."

"Awesome. Can you get my helmet off? I want to smell the sweet, meaty smell of space."

"It's just going to make you hungry," Vicky quipped, tackling his helmet.

"So much the better. It's been, like, twelve hours since we ate anything."

"True."

Derek joined Vicky in the laborious task of getting both his crewmates out of their spacesuits. "We'll have a celebratory feast as soon as you're back in your flight suits."

"Colonel, you're speaking my language. Wow, it does smell like overdone steak. Weird. And delicious! I think I'll have the beef stew."

Once Vicky and Jacob were free and their suits properly stowed, fatigue set in. Jacob scrubbed his face with his hands and Vicky cautiously rotated her right shoulder to make sure it was all right, having felt a slight twinge while getting out of her suit.

"Let's all take some time off," Derek said, noticing the drop in everyone's energy. "You two get cleaned up while I fortify the breach patch. We can fix the tear where the meteorite stopped on the opposite wall, and then call it a night. The entangled particles will be waiting for us tomorrow, and I think we could all use some R & R."

"No argument from me," Jacob said. He yawned, and even Vicky conceded that a little rest would be nice.

Derek reached out and tugged on Vicky's sleeve before she could move toward her locker to retrieve a flight suit.

"Shoulder okay?"

"Oh, yeah. I was just checking. A little strained, maybe," Vicky admitted, glad he hadn't also seen her rotating her wrist. "I was moving and tugging a lot out there when I was stuck. I'm sure Jacob's going to be sore, too, from all the pistol grip work."

Derek nodded, keeping his eyes trained on hers to try and detect any insincerity, but he found none.

"Alright," he said finally. He let go of her sleeve.

Jacob gave her the side-eye as they got cleaned up. "You

didn't really eat one of my chocolate puddings, did you?"

Vicky just looked at him, one eyebrow raised. He broke after only a few seconds, winking at her and smiling as he washed his face with a baby wipe. Vicky shook her head but found herself smiling, too. They'd had a major win that day, despite the difficulties they'd encountered.

"You want to use the bathroom first?" she asked. "You were out there the longest."

"Nah, you go ahead. I'll change out here. Just check before you come back out."

"Okay. Thanks." Vicky grabbed a fresh wet towel and her flight suit and retreated to the tiny bathroom space to wash and change.

"Thanks for joining me." Jeff Marshall sat down with his coffee. Liz had beaten him to the base coffee shop and was sipping on a cold brew in the nearby classified lounge when he arrived.

"Of course."

"How are the simulations going?"

Liz shrugged. "So far, it's pretty consistent; simulations suggest the wormhole likely terminated according to a fractal Random Walk pattern. It's impossible to predict where they might have been deposited in space, although the physicists think they're likely to be somewhere relatively nearby."

"How relatively?"

"Most likely within the Milky Way, maybe even on the same arm. Hopefully not in interstellar space."

Jeff scratched his eyebrow. If they hadn't been deposited near a star they could draw power from, they were already dead.

"Could they be as close as Alpha Centauri?"

"Could be." Liz took another sip of coffee. "There's no way for us to know, even if they're that close—they could be there right now with enough light reflecting off their ship to be detectable from Earth, and we still wouldn't be able to see them."

"Not for another four years, anyway," Jeff said. It would take that long for light to travel to Earth from their hypothetical location in orbit around Alpha Centauri. "They'd be better off to just point the ship toward the sun and start flying our way."

"Except they don't have four years' worth of oxygen onboard. And that's if they were traveling at the speed of light, which they can't do."

"They could scavenge the MSM," Jeff pointed out.

"And get themselves additional food and water, plus nitrogen for the *Pioneer*'s systems," Liz said, nodding. "I thought of that. But they don't have MSM backups for everything. They'll run out of their other consumables with no way to replenish them. They'd run out of their backups before they made it home, too. And that's with them at Alpha Centauri—that's a *best*-case scenario."

"Is that the attitude Simulations is taking?" Jeff guessed, making note of her frustration.

"Basically. Once we verified that they could have gone through an E-R Bridge, we moved very quickly from 'how could they get home' to 'how can we prevent this from happening in the future.'"

"What about, 'how can we get home if this does happen again?'"

Liz shrugged. "We're not there yet." She twirled the straw in her plastic cup. "So I heard they've been declared Missing in Action."

"Yeah." Jeff slouched back in his seat. "We held off as long as we could."

"I was actually surprised how long they waited," Liz admitted. "Did they want to go with 'presumed dead?'"

"A few did," Jeff said. "But we're not ready to go there yet. The particles are still entangled, which means that the ship is still out there, and as long as they didn't run out of power, they've got enough supplies to last them for months—closer to a year if they scavenge the MSM and ration their food, and I don't see why they wouldn't."

"They're pretty resourceful," Liz agreed. She smiled. "No pun intended."

Jeff laughed. "This conversation is bordering on surreal."

They sat in companionable silence for a moment, sipping their drinks and reflecting on the strange reality of what had apparently happened to the *Pioneer*. Liz broke the silence.

"So why did you ask me to meet you here?"

Jeff sat up and leaned forward, bracing his arms on the table. "I want your honest assessment. Could they get themselves home?"

Liz sighed. She really didn't want to think through an answer to that question. "Why are you asking?"

"Because this is the kind of thing we're all going to have to factor in as a risk on future missions, if there are any future missions with the IPS. The decisions I make, and other members of Ground Control, will be affected by what's happened with the *Pioneer*. We all need to start thinking about that, just like the Simulations staff."

Liz nodded her understanding unhappily and looked out the window. Outside, there was a line forming at the coffee shop, mostly uniformed personnel but a few contractors and civilian employees as well.

"Colonel?"

"Yeah." Liz pulled her gaze back to Jeff. "I don't know, Jeff. The science says 'no, they can't'. But it also said that this couldn't happen to begin with. I honestly think that it's possible for them to get back. I just don't see how."

"If travel through a wormhole really does manifest itself in a Random Walk, any attempt to get home could take them anywhere else in space—even farther away."

"With no way to control the process, yes. But what if we worked on it? What if we came up with a way to control it, or at least guide it?"

"Liz, you're talking about science we haven't discovered yet, let alone created equipment and processes to exploit."

"I know, but I think we should be thinking about these things. We're seeing empirical evidence of wormhole creation and travel, and the theory, technology and procedures won't catch up to reality if we don't develop them."

"But without those kinds of developments, it would be pure trial and error."

"And we don't even know if the crew can recreate the conditions because those magnets could get even more out of alignment and change everything. I know. But no matter how improbable, it is still technically possible."

Jeff leaned his cheek on his left fist, elbow on the table.

"So how do we make it more probable?"

Liz spread her hands out in defeat. "They won't let us. All our focus has been put on preventing future wormholes. And I understand why. I do. All other considerations being equal, it's a moot point if we can't talk to the crew. But what about future missions? Isn't this exactly the kind of thing we should be working on in case it *does* happen again?"

"Okay." Jeff sat back in his seat again. "We've been going over similar ground on our end. I'll make your thoughts known in the next meeting."

"Thank you," Liz said. "Thanks for taking the time."

"I can't think of anything more important."

Liz lifted her cup in a silent toast.

Jeff raised his own to join her. "To the crew of the *Pioneer*?"

"To the crew of the *Pioneer*. Wherever they may be."

CHAPTER SEVENTEEN

Derek carefully unscrewed the cover protecting the EPE's computer interface, which consisted of a tablet-sized monitor and fold-out keyboard. It had been thirty-six hours since the EVA ended. The crew had made what repairs they could to the damage caused by the meteorite that had breached the side of the spacecraft, then spent time resting and planning their next move.

Their first task was exposing the computer interface. It was located on the side of the EPE tank, which was filled with liquid nitrogen to keep the experiment at its required super-cold temperatures. The interface itself was designed to be used by future astronauts on NASA's mission to Mars, and the crew of the *Pioneer* had not been briefed on all the capabilities and procedures associated with the EPE and its attached computer.

Derek finally lifted the interface cover from the tank and handed it to Jacob to stow somewhere it wouldn't get in the way.

"Alright. Let's see what we have here." Derek unfolded the thin keyboard and it clicked into place at a ninety-degree angle to the tank. He tapped on the power button that would turn on the monitor and the Linux system immediately came to life. The entanglement program's graphical user interface was open and running.

"Nice," Jacob said softly.

"Are they still entangled?"

Derek poked around the desktop and soon found an icon that opened a status page with green bars indicating that the program was functioning normally.

"There," he said, pointing to a status log at the top of the main program's GUI, with the word "entangled" helpfully highlighted in gray. "Looks like the particles are still entangled. Now let's see if we can open and use MATLAB without disentangling them."

Vicky's notes and Derek's official files about the computer attached to the experiment had told them they needed to run the Mars Protocol in MATLAB, so Derek found and opened the program. He ran a few simple tests to make sure it was working.

"Can you pull up the picture of a dog?"

Derek and Vicky looked at Jacob.

"What dog?" Vicky asked.

"There's a black and white picture of a dog built into MATLAB. You guys didn't know?"

"But of course you do," Vicky said, amused.

"I know a bunch of MATLAB Easter eggs."

"How do I pull it up?"

"May I?" Jacob rotated the experiment, encased in its gray shell, so he could access the fold-out keyboard and type in the lines of code. He grinned when he pressed Enter, rotating the tank back so Derek and Vicky could see. Sure enough, a blue-outlined, pixilated image of a dog's head displayed in a pop-up window.

"It's a husky!"

Derek chuckled. "Very impressive," he said, and they all smiled down at the drawing for a moment before he closed the window. He toggled back to the entangled particles program and found everything as it had been.

"Alright. Now that we've verified that MATLAB is working, even down to the Easter egg level, and it doesn't seem to have affected the experiment, let's see if we can get the Mars Protocol up and running."

Another window popped up, unbidden.

"What's that?" Jacob asked.

Derek studied the window, full of time stamps and 1s, with Vicky peering over his shoulder. "Uh, it looks like a log of measurements on the EPE."

"It makes sense there'd be a log for reference," Vicky said. "The computer at MIT takes a measurement of their Alice particles every ten seconds, and so this computer measures the Bob particles at the same rate, alternating every five seconds. Each time either of us takes a measurement, we change the state of the particles, and that's basically how the computer knows it's all still working. Displaying a log gives visual confirmation."

Jacob pointed at the entries. "Why are they all in orange?"

They pondered the log for a moment, then Vicky suggested that Derek scroll up to see earlier entries. It took a lot of scrolling, but he finally made it to a list of entries in black. The time stamp of the last black entry placed it just before they lost contact with Earth.

Vicky pulled herself closer to see. "These black entries must be the ones that were confirmed by a signal from the Alice computer. The orange ones weren't, because the computers would have lost connectivity once we exited the wormhole, just like we lost link and radio. So the particles are still returning the expected measurements, but there's no independent confirmation."

"Hmm." Jacob crossed his arms. "So the fact that we're still getting ones means MIT is still making their scheduled measurements, right?"

Derek nodded. "That's right."

"Just like we hoped," Vicky said, her eyes bright.

Jacob frowned as a new thought struck. "Which makes it all the more important not to accidentally disentangle the particles."

Derek blew out a long breath. "No pressure, huh?"

"We're working in a totally different program that won't engage the EPE until we tell it to, according to a pre-arranged pattern," Vicky pointed out. "We should be fine."

Derek and Jacob murmured their agreement, but now that they had confirmation that the particles were still entangled and the people on Earth were monitoring them, Vicky had to agree with Jacob. She couldn't shake a sense of unease. It didn't help that she could see it mirrored in the worry lines on Jacob's face and Derek's impassive frown as he got to work, not to mention how difficult retrieving the EPE had turned out to be—and it had primarily been her idea.

The stakes felt enormously high. Continued entanglement may not tell Earth anything more than the fact that the experiment was still in one piece and, by implication, they might be, too, but Vicky couldn't help feeling a growing sense of connection to home, which was irrevocably connected to the particles. She fervently hoped their work on the computer wouldn't interrupt that fragile link.

Derek looked over his shoulder at her. "Abrams, what was the script's name? MarsLab?"

"Yes. It's pre-programmed, so it should come up when you call up the name." She pulled her laptop from its anchorage on the side of the table and opened it to look at the Mars Protocol instructions she'd found.

Derek typed MarsLab into MATLAB and a new graphical user interface window popped up.

Jacob nodded in satisfaction. "Nice. Now all we have to do is input the right commands, right?"

"We should just be pressing buttons in the GUI," Vicky said.

"Here we go," Derek breathed. He hovered the mouse selector over the *Initiate* button.

"Wait!"

Derek pulled his hand away from the mouse pad on the keyboard as Vicky scrutinized the instruction manual. Several seconds ticked by.

"Abrams?"

"Sorry. Go ahead. It's going to ask you for an authentication key. I've got it now."

"Alright." Derek pressed the button and was asked for the key.

Vicky read it aloud while he typed. "Alpha two three two seven, eight five Kilo four Sierra, nine nine one Yankee seven."

Derek read the key back to ensure he hadn't mistyped before pressing the *Enter* button. He was rewarded with a progress bar. "Okay, it looks like it's working."

"How will we know?" Jacob asked.

"The program tells the computer to measure the particles in a specific pattern instead of every ten seconds," Vicky said. "It'll skip some of the measurements. That will create a series of measurement results on the other end that constitute the initialization code. So instead of seeing a line of zeroes, they'll have a sequence of ones and zeroes. If the sequence they see matched the initialization code with ninety percent accuracy or better, they should accept it."

"And we'll see the opposite, right?"

"Correct. We'll see the mirror image instead of the line of ones we normally get."

The progress bar disappeared and a few seconds later, the EPE's measurement log popped up again with a new entry in red.

Jacob crossed his arms. "Red is good?"

"Red means we measured the particles in a spin-up state, corresponding to a zero, which breaks our log of ones," Vicky said. "That's the first mirrored measurement of the initialization sequence."

"So it's working!"

"As far as we know."

Jacob rolled his eyes and Vicky rushed to explain herself.

"Look, I'm sure it's working, but this is where MIT comes in. If they don't realize what's going on right away, they could start troubleshooting and taking extra measurements, or skipping some to test the entanglement—they could interrupt the sequence and never realize we were trying to send them a message. Or they could disentangle the particles altogether."

Derek anchored the experiment to the table by a Velcro strap they'd looped through the small handle on the tank. "Let's hope they give it enough time to recognize the pattern, then. Abrams, does this have a notification system built in?"

"Um...yes." Vicky flipped to the confirmation code page and scanned for the information. "Here it is. The Mars program reads from the EPE log, so it'll beep four times when it detects their complete confirmation code. They may even have a similar function on their end to detect our initialization code."

"Alright. Then let's all get back to work. Mendez, I want you to work on those spectral readings. I'm going to get on that model project we shelved to plan the spacewalk, see if I can build something predictive so we can test out ideas for exerting some control over this wormhole process. Abrams, I believe you're due for your next sleep schedule."

"I'll try to at least get a ballpark of where we are so you can put some starting parameters into your model," Jacob said.

"If I can build the model," Derek hedged. "I have to remember my algorithms first."

"You might not have to." Vicky glided down the habitat to her storage locker. "I have a new e-book on physics on my laptop. It has a section on Brownian motion. I think there may be a chapter on modeling."

Jacob rolled his eyes. "Of course you have a new physics book. Is that what you brought along for your leisure time?"

Vicky just grinned at him. "You brought your favorite episodes of *Stargate* and *Doctor Who*. I brought a bunch of stuff I've been meaning to read. And *Alias*."

"Really? *Alias*? I thought you were more of a documentary nut."

"My interests are varied and nuanced." She pulled her laptop from its bin.

"They're certainly surprising," Jacob muttered, and took his leave of the habitat. Vicky was already absorbed in the task of pulling up the folder containing her e-books.

Paul Brightman opened the door to Ground Control more forcefully than he meant to. He spotted his crewmates immediately—they were all standing around in the aisle by the spaceflight supervisors' desk. Jeff Marshall was on duty, classified phone cradled against his cheek. Paul walked as fast as he could to stand with Liz and James.

"Hey, I just heard. Do we have imagery yet?"

"They've been searching for about two hours," Liz informed him. "They haven't found anything yet."

"Well, it's a big solar system," James said. "I'm just glad they finally approved the telescope resources."

It had been a week since they lost touch with the *Pioneer*, and they'd finally been allowed to reposition a telescope with the capability to search for them in case the wormhole theory was wrong.

"Where are we looking?"

"Right where they should be, according to the flight plan," Liz said. "They're checking the entirety of the flight path since we don't know for sure how long they ran the IPS at a hundred percent. Everything the telescope sees is being run through NASA's supercomputers. They're analyzing every little speck."

"Okay. Thank you very much." Jeff hung up the phone.

He turned to face the crew. "The search of the flight path is complete, although the computers are still analyzing the images."

"Where will they look next?" James asked. "Along the skewed path indicated by the magnet misalignment?"

"Yes."

Paul raised his hand. "Wouldn't they have to look at that path in a 360-degree radius from the *Pioneer*'s last known location?"

"No. The IPS team was able to calculate the directionality of the change in trajectory based on the system's metadata they received before loss of link."

"Wow."

"In the meantime," Liz spoke up, "the three of us should get to work. I called Sims to let them know we'd be late, but we do have to get down there eventually—there's nothing we can do to speed this process up."

"When can we rule out an explosion and put the full force of our efforts behind the wormhole theory?" James asked.

"As soon as we get through this visual search," Jeff said. "Probably in a couple days. And Liz, we managed to convince leadership to let you guys work on return-to-Earth procedures."

Liz broke into a wide smile. "That's excellent news, Flight. Thank you."

"It wasn't just me."

The two officers shook hands and parted ways, Liz leading her team out of Ground Control.

"So what does this mean for us?" James asked. "You know, the whole return-to-Earth thing?"

"It means we can start figuring out how to get the *Pioneer* back."

"But we can't talk to them," Paul pointed out. "So how can we help them?"

"Okay, then, we can figure out how to get ourselves home if we're ever in their shoes. Happy?"

"Not really," Paul admitted. "But I do think the change in focus is good."

"It can only help us," James agreed.

They walked the rest of the way in companionable silence, broken occasionally when they passed other airmen and exchanged verbal greetings and salutes. When they arrived at the Bluebridge Simulations building, they stepped into the air conditioning, removing their hats as they passed through the door frame. They were surprised by the sight of Kevin Thompson casually chatting with the Sergeant on duty at the security desk.

"Major Thompson." Liz greeted him cautiously. Jeff hadn't said anything about him joining them in Simulations. James Archer hung back half a pace as they approached the desk.

"Colonel," Major Thompson said, just as formally. "I'll be working with your team today. Colonel Marshall informed me that the simulations are going to focus on testing the models our physics and IPS departments have been working with. He felt an extra accelerator physicist in the room would be helpful. From now on, I'll be working with the simulators to design and run sims for you three to test out, and acting as a liaison with the IPS team so their extra man in sims can return to work on the theoretical side."

"That's great," James said, stepping forward to shake the major's hand. "Thanks for that."

"Of course."

The Bravo Crew tucked their phones and pocketknives into the lockers in the entry and passed through the metal detectors.

"Is there any news on wreckage?" Major Thompson asked.

Liz shook her head. "We were just in Ground Control. So far the telescope hasn't picked up anything out of the ordinary."

"That is excellent news."

Liz bit back a smile at his formal demeanor. "Yes, it is."

"That should give us extra motivation to be rigorous in our simulations. Doctor Archer."

"Yes?"

"I will be making every effort to ensure accuracy while we test the theory, but if you notice anything amiss, or even have a gut feeling, please don't hesitate to say something. We will consider every comment seriously. Nothing is out of bounds."

James nodded, realizing that in their month apart while he was in Australia with the Charlie Crew, he'd forgotten just how verbose Major Thompson was. "Yeah, no problem."

The major gave him a nod and, as they approached the doorway to the simulated Ground Control room, he bade them goodbye.

"See you on comms," Paul said.

The crew continued down the hall to the next doorway, which led to the spacecraft simulation room.

"Wow," Paul said quietly. "I forgot how . . ."

"Stiff?" James supplied.

"Yeah. I forgot how stiff he is."

"Major Thompson is an excellent officer and a very careful physicist," Liz said, careful to back up her fellow officer even though she couldn't deny their observation.

"No doubt," James said hurriedly. "And it will be helpful to have an IPS astronaut in the sims control room."

He reached their door first and held it open for the other two to enter. Personally, he would have preferred Vicky. He knew Major Thompson would do exemplary work, but he didn't have a shorthand with him like he'd developed with Vicky. James entered the room and walked behind the others toward the huge replica of the *Pioneer* Command Capsule and Habitat Module, and pushed aside his wandering thoughts.

CHAPTER EIGHTEEN

Beep beep beep beep.

Philip turned his phone alarm off and pushed his wheeled chair away from the computer he was working on. He walked around the laser-laden table in the center of the lab and entered the Entanglement Room to check the experiment's log, as he'd been doing every hour for the last three hours. He sat down and logged in to the computer. The log was still open from the last time he'd checked it, so he clicked on it and scrolled up to verify that their measurements were still returning 0s every time as expected. He froze when he saw the first 1s.

"Oh, crap." He scrolled up farther and observed a mess of alternating 1s and 0s; the particles had become disentangled.

"Okay," he said to himself. "Don't panic. Don't panic."

Philip didn't have a clue where the other half of the entangled particles were, or why the experiment had come under such sudden scrutiny the previous week, but he knew that any change to the planned progression of 0s was bad, especially since they'd lost manual confirmation from the Bob particles computer for some reason that hadn't been explained to him. After a few seconds' debate about the appropriate course of action, Philip went back into the main lab and picked up the phone to call Professor Coldwell. She answered on the third ring.

"This is Doctor Coldwell's office; how can I help you?"

"Hi, Doctor Coldwell. It's Philip."

"Hey. What's going on?"

"I'm in the lab. I was just checking the entangled particles, and there are several ones in the log."

Philip waited anxiously for the professor's reply, and it came after only a moment's hesitation.

"I'll be there as soon as I can. Has it settled back down?"

"Uh . . . I think so? I don't know, sorry. I called as soon as I saw the ones."

"That's okay. Check for other instances and make a screen capture of each segment of the log that contains ones. Okay?"

"Yeah, no problem."

"Okay. Bye."

Philip hung up the phone and took a deep breath. The lab was empty save for him, so he had no one to commiserate with until Dr. Coldwell arrived. He went back into the Entanglement Room and started doing what she'd asked. Oddly, there was only one small portion of the log from the last hour that showed anomalous measurements; he even checked back farther than an hour, but it appeared that this was the first instance of an unexpected, unplanned change of state in the particles. He made his screen capture and highlighted every occurrence of a 1 on the copy he printed out, then stood there staring at the paper, his eyes naturally flicking to the monitor as a new entry appeared, on schedule, every ten seconds, until Dr. Coldwell arrived.

"What have we got?"

"Here." Philip handed over the paper and Dr. Coldwell hunched over it, intent on reviewing the data. Philip stuffed his hands in his pockets and tapped his heels while he waited.

"Interesting. Do you have a paper and pen?"

"Uh . . . " Philip looked around and didn't see any. "Hold on, I'll grab some from the other room."

Philip left Dr. Coldwell and rummaged around in his backpack until he found a mechanical pencil. He grabbed a few pieces of paper from the printer and came back to the entanglement room. Dr. Coldwell took the proffered materials and set the blank paper next to the printout of the log on the table. Bending over, she tried to write.

"It's mechanical," Philip murmured.

"Mmmm." Professor Coldwell pushed the button on the side of the pencil to advance the lead and tried again, this time with success. She wrote out the state indicators in sequence horizontally, then straightened up and stared down at her work:

. . . 00000 1 000 111 000 11 00 1 0 1 00 11 000 111 000 1 00000 . . .

Philip squinted at the sequence. "That doesn't look random."

"It's not. It's a palindrome, see? It's the same whether it's read forwards or backwards."

Philip leaned in closer. "Oh, wow. You're right."

"Uh-huh."

"What does that mean?"

Dr. Coldwell tapped the eraser end of the pencil against

the table. "I'm not sure. Could this be a problem with the program on Bob's end? Some sort of glitch or corruption in the code? I'm thinking out loud."

"Well, maybe you should call DARPA. They're the ones who built it, right?"

"Yes." Professor Coldwell was thoughtful. "I was involved in the entanglement process, but they did all the programming. Keep an eye on the log."

"Sure."

Dr. Coldwell picked up the phone and dialed. Philip sat and scrolled back through the log to make sure that they hadn't missed anything while they were focused on the printout.

"Yes, this is Doctor Coldwell at MIT with the entangled particles experiment. Can I speak to one of the project's programmers, please? Yes, I know our log report is almost half an hour late. We've encountered an anomaly. No, I don't know if the particles are still entangled. I think they are, but that's why I need to speak with . . . yes. Yes. Thank you." She turned to Philip. "They're transferring my call."

Philip nodded sagely and turned back to the computer to watch the log.

"Hello, this is Doctor Coldwell at MIT. Hi. Yes, we're getting anomalous measurements on the entangled particles. They seem to be following a pattern. Of course. One, zero, zero, zero. One, one, one. Zero, zero, zero. Then two ones, followed by two zeroes. Then a single one followed by a single zero and another single one. Then two zeroes, two ones, three zeroes, three ones, and a single one. Then the measurements go back to all zeroes, as planned. Yes, I'll repeat the sequence."

She was midway through her repetition of the whole thing when another 1 appeared in the log. Philip had a split-second of uncertainty and decided to wait until she was finished confirming the confusing sequence of 1s and 0s with the person on the other end of the call. As soon as she reached the end, he got her attention and pointed at the computer. She walked over to see, the phone cord hanging between her and the wall.

"Yes, it just started again. Looks like the same sequence. Yes. Alright."

They watched until the log reached the last single 1 and went back to all 0s.

"That's it. It's back to normal now. Mmhm. Yes. It is? You're kidding. For sure? Okay. Yes, I'll be here. Thank you."

Philip watched with raised brows and an open mouth as she hung up the phone.

"Professor?"

Dr. Coldwell turned to face him, regret written on her face. "Philip," she said, "I wish you had the appropriate clearance, because this is huge."

"Really?"

"Yes. Excellent work contacting me as soon as you noticed the change."

Philip blushed a little at the praise. "Thanks. I didn't know what else to do."

"You did exactly the right thing. I really wish I could tell you what's going on."

"So do I," Philip admitted. "But I get it. So . . . is this going to happen every half-hour?"

Dr. Coldwell grimaced. "I can't talk about it. In fact, I'm afraid you have to leave."

"Oh. Really?"

"Really."

Philip and Dr. Coldwell just looked at each other for a moment before Philip realized that she meant right then.

"Oh. Okay. Sorry. Um...do you still need the pencil?"

"No." Dr. Coldwell handed it back to him. "Thank you."

"Yeah. No problem." Philip went back to the main lab and gathered his things, signing off the computer he'd been using. There was no way he'd be able to focus on his class project now. He glanced back at the Entanglement Room before he left, just as Dr. Caldwell closed the door. The lock clicked into place with a sense of finality. Philip sighed. One day he would get the necessary clearance and he would find out just what he'd witnessed. One day.

Jeff Marshall was standing at his desk when he got the call. He'd been on shift for seven hours, trying to wrangle all the departments and all the extra people who were still working on the problem, now dealing with issues of whether the *Pioneer* and its crew could have survived transit through the hypothesized wormhole, how long their life support might last if they had, and now coordinating the visual search between Earth and Mars with NASA, all in an effort to understand what had happened and what might currently be happening aboard the spacecraft. The PR department was still swamped scheduling interviews and fielding questions from the press and the Brown Eyes crew's families about why the crew was officially MIA—a delicate task, given that they couldn't give any classified details.

Meanwhile, leadership was starting to put pressure on Jeff and the other spaceflight supervisors to declare the crew Presumed Dead and move on to preparations for a new manned IPS mission with new safeguards. That was why he needed estimates on how long the crew could survive aboard the *Pioneer*—he and the other spaceflight supervisors had agreed not to declare the crew dead until they were certain they'd reached the end of their resources, and that included taking the extra supplies aboard the MSM into account. Still, when the classified phone at his desk rang, Jeff braced himself for another unpleasant conversation with the wing commander.

"Colonel Marshall, Ground Control Spaceflight Supervisor. How can I help you?"

"Colonel Marshall, this is Barbara Proctor at DARPA."

Barbara's voice on the other end was calm enough, but Jeff immediately recognized a repressed excitement in her tone. He tried to figure out why she might be calling; Barbara was the liaison for multiple programs for NASA and Space Command.

"Hi Barb. Do you have something for us?"

"We're sending you a Doctor Sara Coldwell from the Research Laboratory of Electronics at MIT. She's the senior supervisor of NASA's entangled particles experiment. They're reading her into the *Pioneer* program right now so she'll have the necessary clearance to access Buckley Annex and discuss the mission."

"Okay, slow down for me for a second. Is something going on with the particles experiment? Did they become disentangled?"

"No. The experiment is still running, but Doctor Coldwell recently called to inform us of what appeared to be anomalous readings in the entangled particles log. Her first thought was that the particles may have become disentangled somehow, but she realized that was not the case and called us immediately. In point of fact, the log recorded the initialization code of the Mars Protocol, meant to be sent by the first NASA astronauts to land on Mars."

"Wait. Are you saying the *Pioneer* landed on Mars?"

"Oh, no. No, we are aware that they likely traveled through an E-R Bridge to another part of the galaxy or beyond. What I'm saying is that DARPA and NASA have determined that only a human actor could have instructed the computer with the Bob particles—the ones we sent into space with the *Pioneer*—to begin the initialization sequence. Only a human could have done that. Which means that at least two members of the crew are still alive, or were at the time that they performed an EVA to retrieve the experiment from the MSM and initialized the program."

Jeff rubbed his forehead, not yet ready to buy into what she was saying in case he was misunderstanding. "So . . . we have proof they're alive?"

"Yes. We have proof they're alive, sent to us on purpose by the crew themselves."

Jeff sighed and blinked back tears of relief. "That is outstanding news," he said, his voice choked. "Thank you for calling."

"Well, there's a bit more to it than that. If the crew has the experiment, we can communicate using the pre-planned procedures. But we might also be able to figure out some way to communicate more meaningfully, to send more complex messages back and forth. We'll have to put our heads together for that, so we're sending the experiment and Dr. Coldwell to you. You should be hearing from NASA as well."

"That sounds great! When will Doctor Coldwell arrive?"

"She'll be on a flight in four hours. We've already sent her itinerary to your squadron headquarters, and we'll be faxing over her clearance verification and a copy of the signed non-disclosure agreement as soon as her read-in is finished. She should be ready to come in first thing in the morning."

"Okay. Thank you so much, Barb. Is there anything else?"

"Nope. That's all."

"Well, you've made my day. Thanks for the call. Have a good one."

"You, too."

Jeff hung up the phone and took a moment to just breathe. Confirmation. The crew was alive. They were alive and they'd taken the initiative to retrieve the experiment from the MSM. They had used it to communicate the fact of their continued existence, and Barbara had sounded optimistic about the possibility of further, additional communication. It was almost too much to take in. He looked around the room at the busy airmen and civilians, working hard to solve an unsolvable problem, and swallowed back a fresh wave of tears.

"Everybody listen up," he said, loud enough to get their attention. He waited until everyone was looking his direction before speaking again.

"I just got off the phone with DARPA. We just got proof of life for the crew of the *Pioneer*—at least two of them." A murmur of excitement, astonishment, and disbelief interrupted him for a moment, but he held up his hands and the room turned pin-drop silent.

"DARPA just got the Mars astronaut code from the entangled particles experiment. Now, the only way that's possible is if someone went out to the MSM and brought the experiment back to the *Pioneer*, where they initiated the code meant to be used by the first astronauts on Mars. They're alive, and they're talking to us."

Ground Control erupted. Everyone seemed to be clapping, cheering, and hugging each other all at once. For a long moment, the room was plunged into ecstatic, joyous chaos. The flight activities officer was weeping openly, and Jeff's eyes brimmed again when the flight surgeon wrapped his arms around the man. As the din subsided, Jeff called for order once again.

"Alright, alright. Settle down. Here's the deal: We all still have jobs to do—nothing changes about that. We still need to know how long they can survive. But now we know they're still out there, alive and kicking. So let's do our best for them."

The room went back to work in a buzz, and Jeff sat down. He needed to call Liz and the Charlie Crew commander, not to mention the wing commander. But for now, Jeff gave himself a moment. He wiped away the tears that were finally falling with trembling hands. He couldn't stop smiling.

CHAPTER NINETEEN

Derek was reviewing the digital physics book Vicky had brought with her to find an algorithm he needed to build his model, wishing he'd had the foresight to put his ebook copy of *Numerical Recipes in C* on his laptop, when the EPE computer beeped, informing him that there was activity in the MarsLab script. He reached over to pull the experiment around so that he could see the monitor, his heart thumping in anticipation. He checked his watch and pulled the keyboard into place. The timing was spot-on.

"Mendez! Abrams!"

Vicky fumbled with the buttons and straps of the treadmill she was running on while Jacob glided in from the Command Capsule.

"Is it them?"

"Maybe." Derek turned on the screen and scrutinized the MarsLab GUI. A small popup window stated that a Mars Protocol Command Code had been recognized. Derek clicked on the popup's *Display* button and the three crew members huddled around the screen to see. A log entry appeared in the GUI to alert them that the Mars Protocol confirmation code had been recognized.

"Yes!" Derek said, pumping his fist and then slapping

his knees like a drummer. Vicky grabbed her head with both hands, grinning madly, and still breathing a little heavily from her workout. Jacob let out a loud, long *woop* that had Vicky shifting her hands to cover her ears.

"Haha!" he shouted. "Whip me, beat me, take away my charge card—NASA is talking! It's NASA! Whoa!"

Derek and Vicky stared as he clumsily attempted a backflip, their smiling faces frozen. Derek shifted first, his brows crinkling in obvious confusion, which Jacob realized was not an expression he'd ever seen on the man's face before. Vicky looked concerned for his sanity.

"You've got to be kidding. You've never seen *Space-Camp*? Did you miss that movie night during Candidate School? It's a classic! Okay. Team movie night. I've got it on my laptop—don't ask me how—and I am going to initiate the two of you into the wonder and joy that is 1980s family sci-fi drama, okay? We'll break open some lemonade drink packs, we'll dig into the candy-coated almonds—it'll be like a movie theater. I can't believe neither of you have seen it."

Derek shook his head in silent judgement of Jacob's mania, but Vicky's concerned look had evolved back into a smile. She giggled a little and snorted, which set them all off. At Jacob's instigation, they linked arms and twirled awkwardly in the middle of the module until they were dizzy and breathless from their giddy laughter.

"Alright, alright," Derek said as they caught their breath. "That's enough. We all still have work to do—this isn't a movie, after all."

Vicky snickered and headed back for the treadmill. Jacob surveyed his teammates.

"You two are unbelievable. You know that? You're no

fun at all. But we're gonna do it," he called over his shoulder as he headed back to the Command Capsule. "We're gonna have movie night! Then you'll know!"

"Can't wait," Derek called after him, deadpan. Jacob's head and shoulders emerged from the tunnel and he pointed wordlessly at his commander.

"You'll see," he promised. "You'll all see."

"Whatever floats your boat," Vicky called from the gym.

"Go back to work, Mendez. I'll let you know if anything else happens."

"Okay. But when you're both laughing at Tish and crying with Max, I'll have the last laugh."

Derek tossed a bag of water in his direction and Jacob disappeared. He smiled at his junior officer's antics, but sobered quickly as they passed through a particularly dense micrometeorite storm. He almost held his breath as the tiny rocks continued to ping against the side of the spacecraft. More than once he heard a *plunk*. Finally they were out of it and all he could hear was the hum of the ship and the airflow between the fans to the CO_2 scrubbers. It took some effort to refocus on his model-building.

Derek yawned, even as he found the algorithm he needed in Vicky's book. Astronauts routinely suffered from lack of sleep, and he was certainly feeling it that day. It was as if he was finally crashing after more than a week of crisis. His vision was blurrier than usual, too, which he hoped was just a result of his fatigue. There was always the possibility that he was beginning to experience visual impairment intracranial pressure. Plenty of astronauts suffered from VIIP to various degrees—it was one of the drawbacks to spending prolonged periods of time in space, and they all had reading glasses with them in case any of them developed symptoms during the long flight, but none of them wanted to need them. Derek sighed and checked the time. It was just past two in the morning, Zulu, which was the Air Force's brevity code for Greenwich time; two hours later than he was supposed to have tucked himself into their tiny shared bedroom to try to sleep for a few hours.

No wonder his vision was suffering—he'd been staring at computer screens for nearly thirteen hours. Derek rubbed his face and shut down the laptop. It would be there when he woke up. He went through his end-of-day routine, capped with the consumption of a sleep aid, and closed the bedroom door behind him. He put his earbuds in and turned on some cool jazz to help him drift off before pulling the sleep sack around him, putting his arms through the arm holes and zipping it up. Finally, he turned out the light and prayed that sleep would come quickly and linger for more than the two or three hours he tended to get. Derek breathed in deeply and let it out slowly, trying to clear his head. He was asleep in seconds.

He was awake in minutes.

The breach alarm cut through the soft music piping into Derek's ears. He breathed in without a thought. Since he was not free to move immediately, he followed procedure and reached for the little room's emergency oxygen kit, putting it on and activating it before extracting himself from the sleep sack. He emerged from the bedroom and took in the situation at a glance.

At the back of the Habitat Module, Vicky was similarly extracting herself from the treadmill straps, oxygen mask on. Jacob was nowhere to be seen. A segment of the wall was lit in blue near the table, which was also—Derek's heart skipped a beat—near one of their oxygen tanks. He made his way to the point, fishing a FastPatch out of his pocket just as Vicky got out of the treadmill apparatus. She joined him and together they searched the compromised area for a hole. Vicky found it first, a small tear near the left edge of the segment. She probed the hole, but couldn't tell if it had damaged anything else, so she took the appropriately small FastPatch that Derek held out to her and applied it, mentally lining the tear up with the craft's layout. It was about four inches from the oxygen tank; depending on the angle of impact, it could have hit the tank.

The blue light on the panel blinked out as the patch sealed the hole, but the red ship-wide lights kept flashing and the alarm continued to blare. There was a half-second of confusion before Vicky and Derek's eyes met in realization: they had more than one breach.

The two of them scoured the habitat, looking for an exit point for the projectile that had created the tear they'd found, but there were no more blue lights anywhere to be seen. Derek snagged Vicky's sleeve and pointed to a smudge on the ceiling as the lights and siren finally shut off. They inspected the smudge and found that it obscured a nick about the same size of the tear they had plugged.

Vicky found the offending piece of shrapnel floating near the floor. It looked about the right size to have caused both the tear and the nick and, judging from the angle between those two points, it would have missed the oxygen tank. She gave Derek a thumbs-up and he nodded his understanding and agreement. She signed the letter M at chin level, toggling her hand back and forth a little in shorthand for *Mendez*. While the NASA astronauts had been learning Russian to communicate with their foreign teammates in the International Space Station program, the Air Force had taught their people some American Sign Language so that they could communicate nonverbally if they needed to. It was one of several protocols NASA was considering implementing for their own long-term space-flight missions to the moon and Mars. Now the crew of the *Pioneer* could report back that it had come in handy.

Derek signed back his intention to check on Jacob in the Command Capsule and indicated that Vicky should check for other damage in the habitat, just in case. She complied immediately, moving to the front of the module to begin a careful sweep with a handheld Ultrasonic Leak Detector that could find leaks too small for the ship-wide system to catch, and Derek glided to the front of the habitat and through the access tunnel to the capsule.

Jacob was there, busy fortifying a manual patch to the ceiling just above Derek's window, covering it with duct tape. Derek frowned at the sight. It must have been some hole to prompt him to tape an area the size of a basketball. He tapped Jacob on the shoulder and the younger man greeted him with a grunt, then pointed to Vicky's window. The meteorite had gone right through the thick plastic, crossed the capsule, and exited above Derek's window. If he hadn't been wearing an oxygen mask, Derek would have whistled. As it is, he knew Jacob needed help fortifying his patch jobs, so Derek retrieved another roll of tape and started working on Vicky's window.

When they were finally through, Derek stored the tape while Jacob checked their status on Derek's computer readouts. Derek returned to look over his shoulder. The pressure was still too low to take off their oxygen masks, but it was rising. Jacob grunted and pointed at the power gauge. Derek's stomach dropped when he saw it. The needle was going down again.

"So they sent the initialization code and we sent the confirmation code. What comes next?"

Paul consciously did not drum his fingers on the table. He was happy that they had proof of life for the crew, but it only made him more eager to be in the simulator, actively working the problem. Instead, he was stuck in a meeting with Jeff Marshall, representatives from NASA and DARPA, and the professor who'd been monitoring the experiment from MIT. She answered his question.

"The program will run its course unless willfully interrupted. There are several more planned exchanges of code to test our working probability models and other connectivity and interpretive issues."

Paul could feel his face scrunching up, but he couldn't seem to stop it. "What does that mean, though? For the mission as it currently stands."

Dr. Coldwell pursed her lips. "Not much, I'm afraid. We have our proof of life, such as it is, and now we have to wait for the program to complete running its operations. If we interrupt it, we could confuse the crew, or even disentangle the particles."

"So meaningful communication ended after we sent the confirmation code," Liz clarified.

"No. No, not quite. All communication is meaningful," Dr. Coldwell corrected her. "Even these codes told us the crew of the *Pioneer* are alive, and hopefully the fact that we sent the confirmation code told them that we understood their message."

"Okay, maybe 'meaningful' wasn't the best word," Liz amended with far more patience than Paul could have mustered. "But what potential is there for further communication? Something beyond the initialization program?"

Dr. Coldwell shook her head. "The problem lies in verification. You see, the Alice and Bob particles—that's what we call the particles at either end of the experiment—are entangled, so any change to one set affects a corresponding, mirror-image change to the other. We can't know the state of the particles until we measure them, but the very act of measuring them changes their state."

James propped his head up with his palms under his chin and Paul resisted the urge to slump in his chair. He hated quantum physics.

Dr. Coldwell went on explaining. "But changes of state can happen at random as well—that's why MarsLab is programmed to accept the prearranged signals with a ninety percent accuracy instead of demanding a hundred percent. But the only way to know for certain that the state we measure was caused by a corresponding, earlier measurement of the Bob particles, is if someone with the Bob particles tells us so using normal communication channels. Hence the pre-planned exchanges. With the time delay for that signal increasing the farther the Bob experiment traveled from Earth, and the possibility that the signal could become corrupted or the information in it otherwise lost, we had to design the experiment to accept unverified but as-expected state changes to the particles, which we decided to measure every alternating ten seconds on both ends of the experiment for maximum data sets. In short, at five seconds after the hour, the computer on the *Pioneer*'s experiment takes a measurement, and at ten seconds after the hour, ours does, and so on. If that chain of events remains unbroken, the Bob particles should always register as ones and the Alice particles, the ones we have, should register as zeroes."

Paul stole a look at James, but the accelerator physicist was listening intently, scribbling notes on a scrap of paper in handwriting too messy for Paul to read.

"We had a delayed verification process because of the limitations of the speed of light in sending a signal from the Bob computer to the Alice computer," Dr. Coldwell went on. "But we had reasonable belief that the particles were still entangled even after the *Pioneer* disappeared, because everything was proceeding as planned. The crew interrupted the sequence with the initialization code, but because that too was prearranged, we recognized it for what it was without needing verification. Any attempts to communicate in a way that has not been pre-planned cannot be relied upon because, with the *Pioneer* potentially on the other side of the galaxy, we won't get the signal from the Bob computer for hundreds or thousands of years, so verification that we are receiving what they mean to send us is impossible."

The Bravo Crew stared at her.

"That didn't help me at all," James admitted.

"And it isn't helping the crew of the *Pioneer*," Paul said. "If we can't communicate meaningfully with them, and I stress 'meaningfully,' then why are we even talking about this? We should be in the simulators figuring out how to get them home."

Liz leaned back in her chair. "So let me see if I understand this. Basically, even though state changes between the two sets of particles are instantaneous because they're entangled, using them to send ad hoc messages is problematic because the verification signals have to follow the laws of physics—no faster-than-light communication."

"That is correct," Dr. Coldwell said.

"So that's why we're here. To find a way around that issue."

"Precisely."

Paul looked back and forth between them. "Okay, I'm lost."

"Oh." Next to him, James put his arms down on the table. "I get it. All this 'no verification,' 'preplanned' stuff is predicated on the requirements of scientific studies. You have to be able to support your findings by verifying everything in order to publish. But this is no longer academic for us—there's nothing stopping us from experimenting freely."

"Right," Liz said, and Paul slumped in his chair.

"Finally, somebody who speaks English. So what can we do?"

Jeff capped the pen he'd been taking notes with. "We propose putting Charlie Crew in the simulator now that they're all back from Australia. They can work on figuring out how to get the *Pioneer* home. Liz, you and Paul will shift to concentrate on this communications problem with Dr. Coldwell and the entanglement team from NASA. Together, you will develop procedures for non-verifiable communication via the entangled particles, which will be simulated, and implemented."

It was Liz's turn to be unhappy. "You want to take us off troubleshooting a return protocol?"

"Charlie Crew is perfectly capable of running the sims," Jeff said, "and they'll be working with the IPS team and the physicists—and Major Thompson. But this is the new Crewcom, and that's Bravo Crew's number-one priority. Besides," he added, "you two both know at least one member of Brown Eyes very well."

The two of them shared an involuntary smile: Vicky.

"Presumably," Jeff finished, "you can get inside their heads and figure out what method of communication is most likely to make sense to them."

"He's right," Liz said quietly for Paul's and James' benefit. Jeff could order them to do it but she noticed he hadn't. He wanted them to choose it.

"Flight," James said, his tone troubled. "I've been working with Colonel Fischer and Major Brightman for the past week, ever since I got back from Australia. They've already lost one mission specialist. I'd like to see this through with them."

Liz was surprised at how his simple statement choked her up. She looked at Jeff and nodded her agreement.

"Very well," Jeff said, his voice full of understanding. "I'll assign Major Thompson to Charlie Crew for the remainder of the mission."

"Thank you, sir," James said quickly. Paul and Liz shared a warm look and Paul slapped James awkwardly on the shoulder. Somehow, without consciously trying, they'd become a team.

CHAPTER TWENTY

The crew of the *Pioneer* floated together in the Command Capsule, trying and failing to ignore the *pings* of micrometeorites colliding with the spacecraft. The dust storms had grown more frequent than ever, and after their triple breach, they all tensed up at the slightest sound.

Once they'd fortified all three patch jobs, Derek had ordered a thorough inspection of the craft's interior using hand-held ULDs to check for leaks too small to trip the system. They'd started in the Command Capsule, closing the hatch to the Habitat Module to isolate the area, then they'd moved on to the habitat, which they'd in turn isolated from the Command Capsule. They'd found a tiny hole one millimeter in diameter inside the airlock and patched it, but they were satisfied that the rest of the craft was secure.

Derek and Jacob inspected the exterior as well, looking for damage via the cameras mounted outside the ship, while Vicky powered the Habitat Module back down to Protocol Three to save power. They found a lot of surface damage, but what worried Derek was the visible damage to their main solar array: One of the panels was bent at an awkward angle and those around it were pockmarked.

Another panel was practically shredded; it would have to be replaced altogether.

Derek did a lot of analyzing and thinking while they worked, and once the inspections were complete, he called a team meeting.

"Clearly," he began, "we're flying through a particularly dirty part of space. So let's take stock. We've now had two breach incidents resulting in a total of four major breaches, plus one minor breach, a cracked lens on exterior camera four, and significant damage to segments seven and ten of our main solar array. Conclusion: we can't stay here."

Jacob and Vicky nodded their agreement and kept quiet as Derek continued.

"We have to get out of this area, but Mendez thinks it's a nebula, which I'm inclined to agree with at this point, and nebulas are, in a word, big. The only way we can get clear is by using the IPS to create another E-R Bridge. Questions, comments, concerns?"

Jacob raised his hand. "I have a question. Assuming that we came here through a wormhole created by the Hawk-E, which we seem to be committed to now, yes?"

"Yes."

"Okay. Assuming that, we're also assuming that the IPS will create another wormhole if we fire it up again. But we can't know that for sure. Right?"

Derek looked to Vicky, who answered with some hesitation.

"Not for sure, no. Theoretically, it should work just like last time. The problem is stability."

"Stability? Like, to avoid an explosion?"

"No, I'm talking about the stability needed to recreate the conditions that made this possible. The Hawking Engine is basically just a particle accelerator running in reverse time. The photons are sent through tiny manufactured black holes to create Hawking radiation, which propels the craft forward. Now, that's an oversimplification, but regardless, the key element for propulsive purposes is the magnets. They direct the flow of the matter and anti-matter, separating them and sending the antimatter out the back of the accelerator while diffusing the matter all around so that it neither cancels out the antimatter nor creates a resistive wall of matter in front of the ship."

"Yeah, that sounds oversimplified to me," Jacob said, raising one eyebrow in an impressive imitation of Stephen Colbert.

Vicky spared him a dark glance and pressed on. "If we created a stable Einstein-Rosen Bridge, we did it by compressing the matter in the front of the ship—which could only have existed in sufficient density if the magnet misalignment sent it forward—that's the only explanation I can come up with. The magnets would have had to come out of alignment enough to shift the matter emitted by the accelerator from a diffusion pattern to a stream aimed more or less toward the front of the craft, which is supported by the Caution and Warning reports in the IPS data. That would have provided enough matter for us to compress, especially given our acceleration at the time and the fact that the IPS was operating at a hundred percent capacity. But that would have required a significant shift in the alignment, which means the magnets may have actually become unseated, although that's something I have not been able to verify."

"Okay," Derek held his hand up to stop her. "What's our bottom line?"

"If the magnets are unseated, as I think they must be, we can't control their positioning. It is an inherently unstable situation. We have no way of controlling what they'll do if we turn the IPS back on, let alone operate anywhere close to full capacity. They could shift back to where they're supposed to be. They could also become even more misaligned and trip the failsafe so the engine shuts itself off and won't engage again."

Derek steepled his fingers and processed the information. Eventually they would have to risk using the IPS anyway to get home. They'd just be testing it out early.

"We don't have a choice," he decided. "If we stay here, we'll die the death of a thousand cuts and the IPS is our only ticket out of here. Is there anything we can do to stabilize the magnets?"

"Not if we want to create a wormhole. There's nothing I can do from here except try to realign them. That didn't work last time, but if I tried it again and it did work, they would no longer be in place to create that wall of matter in front of us."

"What about another EVA?" Jacob asked.

Vicky shot that one down, too. "I can only make superficial repairs to the IPS. Anything beyond the outer layers would have to be done in a clean room with specific tools that we don't have."

Jacob crossed his arms and looked away. Vicky's peremptory dismissal of his idea annoyed him, but he couldn't argue with the facts.

Derek unsteepled his fingers and let his hands hover

over the table. "Then we'll just have to try it and hope for the best. We'll have to do it soon, too. We're still losing power, even with Protocol Three in place."

"Sir, why don't you let me and Vicky go out and fix the solar array?"

Derek was shaking his head before Jacob finished asking. "No. I'm not sending either of you out there again for anything short of a catastrophic emergency repair."

"You sent us out before," Jacob argued.

"That was before I knew the full extent of the danger. We hadn't experienced a single hull breach or taken any noticeable damage yet. You're not going out there," Derek said firmly. "We are using the IPS to create a wormhole so we can get out of this nebula. Then and only then will we plan a spacewalk for repairs to the solar array. This is not up for debate."

They ruminated in silence for a moment, and Vicky surprised Derek by speaking up first.

"We'll need to mitigate," she said, her voice and demeanor decisive. "I'll work on an acceleration procedure to get us to a hundred percent as fast as possible without causing any kind of jolt forward, to reduce the chances of the magnets shifting more."

"I'll try to figure out if there's anything we can do to try controlling the wormhole, even a little bit," Jacob offered. "Oh, and I should grab the video camera so I can get some footage of the stars as we go through the wormhole. That might help me figure out where we go relative to where we currently are."

"Good idea," Derek said. "Vicky, I want to know exactly how much power we need to run the IPS long enough to get out of here—the gauge needle is dropping faster than I'd like so for now, let's assume we only have hours to make this happen."

"We probably do only have hours," Vick said. "The IPS will start creating some of its own charge once it's up to twenty-five percent, but it uses a lot of power to initialize and get to that point."

"Then let's get to it."

They broke with one accord. Derek went back into the now-dark Habitat Module to grab caffeine pills and water for all of them. In the Command Capsule, Jacob unstowed the video camera and anchored it to the ceiling above his seat, so that it was aimed out his navigational window. Once he was happy with its position, he took his steno pad out of his calf pocket and flipped to an empty page to start jotting down some ideas about controlling their wormhole. Next to him, Vicky powered up her laptop to crunch the numbers to determine the power requirements for the IPS. Another wave of micrometeorites hit the *Pioneer* and Vicky pressed her lips together and forced herself to stay on task. She resisted the temptation to look at her taped-up window. They couldn't afford to be worried—they didn't have time.

Paul heaved a sigh, confident that nobody would hear it. There were twenty-two people jammed into the conference room arguing about the best way to try sending an intelligible message to the crew of the *Pioneer* using the entangled particles. At the moment, it was James versus Stephanie

Andrews, a linguist assigned to the program from Indiana University.

James was saying that Morse code was the best means of communication they had at their disposal, but Stephanie was having none of it.

"You cannot tell me the best we can do is Morse code."

"Morse code is simple," Dr. Coldwell pointed out thoughtfully. "It's a pulse—on, off. A binary system is perfect for it—it's essentially just ones and zeroes anyway."

"And the crew are all proficient," James added. "They'll figure it out right away."

"It's an incredibly inefficient way to communicate," Stephanie countered. "It will take forever to tell them anything."

"We're not looking for efficiency. We're just trying to communicate, period."

Stephanie crossed her arms. "And when you want to say more than 'do you copy?' What then? The computers are only taking measurements every ten seconds. That's too slow. We need to think outside the box on this one."

"We are thinking outside the box—nobody's done this before. Complex communications via entangled particles is a new thing."

"Okay." Liz's command voice cut through the tension and even stopped Stephanie with her mouth open to reply. Liz waited a beat and continued in a more regulated tone.

"From where I sit, you both have valid points. Why don't we look at this in stages instead of treating it as a zero-sum game?"

Stephanie squinted at Liz. "Such as?"

"Stage One: establishing communications. For that, we

can use Morse code—keep it simple to increase the likelihood that they'll recognize it for what it is. Stage Two: increase efficiency. We'll develop another means of communicating, something more efficient than Morse code so we can exchange more complex information in a shorter amount of time."

"We could use Morse to communicate the new method to the crew," Paul jumped in quickly. "We also need a way to tell them when we're finished with an instruction or question. Presumably we'll need a schedule so we don't talk over each other and mess everything up. We'll have to communicate that as well."

James scowled. "So even using Morse to start isn't going to be so simple."

"Why don't we break up into teams?" Liz suggested.

Dr. Coldwell nodded eagerly. "I can head up a team to figure out an effective schedule and a method of conveying that to the crew."

"And Doctor Andrews can lead the team working on alternate means of communicating," Liz said, her tone making it a suggestion rather than an order. Stephanie nodded agreement.

"Do we need anything else?" Paul asked, afraid they would miss something in their eagerness to get started.

Everyone sat in silence for a moment, scouring their brains for any angle they may have overlooked.

"If anyone thinks of anything else," Liz said when nobody spoke up, "let me know. In the meantime, Paul, I want you on Doctor Andrews' team; James, you're with Doctor Coldwell. That way we'll have one person on each team who knows the crew and our existing communication protocols."

The group split up, taking position at the white boards on opposite ends of the room. The physicists went with Dr. Coldwell while the linguists and most of the computer scientists went with Stephanie. Liz pulled Paul aside.

"Hey, I need to go give Flight an update and check in with Simulations and squadron leadership. Let me know if you guys make any breakthroughs, okay?"

"Will do."

Liz left and Paul turned his attention to Stephanie, who was writing two numbers on the white board: two and thirty-six.

"This," she said, pointing to the "two", "is now many states we have to work with. This," pointing to the "thirty-six", "is how many letters and numbers we have to convey, to say nothing of symbols. A measurement is taken every five seconds by one half of the experiment or the other; ten seconds on each side. That cannot change without risk of information warping. So. How do we see past all these parameters? Any ideas?"

It was quiet for a few seconds, then Paul spoke up. "James had a point. We have to communicate in binary. What system is better than Morse for our purposes?"

"Bacon's Cipher, for one," Stephanie retorted. She wrote a series of 1s and 0s on the board:

101010 000 111011101110 000 10101

"That's SOS in the simplest possible binary from of Morse code. Morse is really a three-point system, so it takes forever to transmit in binary. That's twenty-nine digits, or 290 seconds. Almost five minutes just to send these three letters. On the other hand, this," she continued, writing again, "is SOS in Bacon's Cipher."

10001 01111 10001

Paul whistled low in surprise. "That's one, two...nine ...fourteen characters shorter than Morse code binary, more than two minutes faster to send!"

"That's right. But I think we can do even better. We have to do better than this. So consider this the brainstorming phase. Let's start throwing ideas on the pile."

On the other side of the room, James was shooting down a suggestion for a communications schedule he thought was too fast.

"We need to keep in mind that the crew is not expecting us to do this," he said. "It might take them a while to figure out what's happening when we send our first message, and then decipher the message itself. And once we've established two-way comms, we'll need them to relay some relatively complex information. They're going to need time, and I don't want to rush them—that's how mistakes are made. We need to build in more time than we think is necessary on both our ends—we can always compress the schedule later."

The man who'd made the suggested timetable didn't look happy, but he didn't argue.

"Doctor Archer is right," Dr. Coldwell said. "Even the act of sending each message in Morse will take a significant amount of time, given the constraints of the alternating ten-second measurement schedule."

James crossed his arms. He hoped the other team would

somehow manage to come up with a more efficient means of communication and figure out how to tell the crew about it, because he was doing the math in his head and as much as he hated to admit it, communicating in binary Morse was going to be a headache. He pinched the bridge of his nose—he was already getting one.

CHAPTER TWENTY-ONE

Vicky reviewed the procedure she had just decided on to get the IPS up to a hundred percent capacity as fast as the system and the crew would tolerate. She had decided the simplest method was "hand-flying" the craft, switching the engine controls to manual shortly after engagement so she could effect a hopefully smooth, continual increase at a pace she could control instead of the normal method of stair-stepping their acceleration up. The engine had manual controls in case the automation failed, but they were not meant to be used for a continuous increase maneuver; Vicky was going to find out how steady her hands were. Satisfied that the procedure would work without shorting anything out, she calculated how much power they would need, and her eyes widened as she realized how much it would take.

"Hey, Jacob? What's our current power level?"

Jacob held up his index finger while he finished balancing a formula in his notepad.

"Now, Jacob."

He looked up at the uncharacteristic demand and saw the urgency in her eyes. "Um, forty-five percent," he said, checking the gauge on Derek's console.

Vicky swore softly. Their power was dropping faster

than she'd realized—there was no time to discuss their options. She only hesitated for a moment before taking the initiative and grabbing her IPS checklist. "Colonel!"

Next to her, Jacob jumped at the volume of her yell. "What's going on?" he asked as she started powering up the IPS without approval.

"We only have about twenty-two minutes to get the IPS up to a hundred percent and let it run for a bit before shutdown. Less, if we want to have any power left to live on afterward."

Derek appeared from the tunnel. "What's happening?"

"Apparently we have to do this right now," Jacob said, putting his notebook away and checking to make sure the video camera was still in place.

Derek got into his seat without hesitation. "Everybody strap in. Start the IPS checklist," he said, even though Vicky was already on step eight, "but hold on the final step. Mendez, any idea how long we need to be in the wormhole to get out of the nebula?"

"No clue, sir. I didn't get that far."

"Give me a guess."

"Uh, twenty seconds. If we're 600 lightyears from home and we were in the wormhole for about a minute last time, which I don't think we were, but . . . twenty seconds should be plenty to get out of the nebula. Hopefully. More if we want to try to get back home."

"One problem at a time. Abrams? How long can we run the IPS on our power supply once we're in the wormhole?"

"Shorter is better," she said tersely, inputting numbers and flipping switches fast enough to make Jacob nervous she might accidentally skip a step.

"When will you be ready?"

"Almost there. I'm going to have to run it manually, by the way."

Jacob and Derek both looked over at Vicky upon hearing that revelation, but she was focused and didn't notice. They exchanged a glance and Jacob tightened his seat straps.

"Roger," Derek said grimly.

Vicky moved through the steps as fast as she could, aided by the fact that she had the sequence memorized. She finally made it to the last step and just managed to catch herself before completing it.

"Ready!"

"Oxygen," Derek said.

Jacob reached out and flipped the switch that turned on the capsule's emergency oxygen supply and they donned the accompanying oxygen masks. Derek had decided they should wear the masks during the maneuver in case of breaches while they increased their velocity, and the capsule's built-in system had mics attached to the masks, meaning they'd still be able to talk to each other.

Derek checked that Vicky and Jacob had their masks on before giving the order. "Engage IPS."

Vicky hit the button. "Engaging IPS. Executing manual override."

"Execute!"

Overriding the automated system was a three-step sequence that ended with Vicky punching in her authorization code. She almost mistyped but managed to hit the right buttons on the touch screen, and was granted manual control of the system. She wrapped her left hand around the throttle and suddenly realized she hadn't strapped in yet—

she'd been working through her checklist. With gritted her teeth, she pushed her feet farther into the floor grips.

"Accelerating now," she said. Derek acknowledged the report and Vicky began to push the lever controlling their rate of acceleration forward as she fumbled with the seat straps with one hand. Jacob saw what she was doing and loosened his own straps so he could reach out and help her. Together, they managed to get her straps buckled, if not tightened, while she controlled the increase in their velocity as smoothly as she could manage.

"Twenty-five percent," Vicky said, and gave Jacob a nod of thanks. The number and volume of *pings* from meteorites increased as they accelerated.

"This is eating up a lot of power," Derek said. "Are you sure we have enough?"

"Yes, sir," Vicky said, even though she wasn't sure at all. She had done the math, but she'd done it quickly and hadn't had anyone check it. She could have made a mistake. Vicky fought back a moment of panic. It was too late now. They were committed.

"Fifty percent!" she said. "I'm going to increase a little faster."

"Do it."

Jacob groaned in his seat between then. He was starting to feel the pull of the G-forces. It was already making him nauseated again, which had the added bonus of reminding him of how sick he'd gotten when they'd entered the wormhole and the stars had started jumping around. And in their rush, nobody had thought to take any anti-nausea medicine before Vicky started up the IPS.

The red lights of the breach alarm system flashed. Vicky

gritted her teeth, the high-pitched, intermittent tone blaring in her ears, almost covering up the now-near-constant meteorite impacts.

"Eighty percent. Eighty-five. Ninety percent. Whoa!"

Jacob looked over at her and immediately wished he hadn't. Out her window, around the taped-up breach patch, the stars were already moving, swooping around the ship like before.

"Hold here!" Derek ordered while Jacob scrambled for a barf bag and ripped it open to hold to his face in pessimistic anticipation.

Vicky stilled her hand on the throttle, starting to feel nauseous herself. Seeing Jacob's preparations in her peripheral vision wasn't helping. Her one consolation was that the meteorite impacts had ceased as soon as they entered the wormhole, leaving them only with the persistent blaring of the breach alarm.

"Holding at ninety-three percent!" she reported.

"Prepare for emergency shutdown!"

Vicky almost took her hand off the throttle—the emergency shutdown switch was on the same side as the lever and she couldn't reach it with her right hand.

"Jake!"

Jacob looked over, the bag still covering most of his face. The stars blinking in and out beyond Vicky made his head swim and he closed his eyes and breathed desperately.

"I need your help with the shutdown!"

Jacob understood in an instant and reopened his eyes, mercifully having to look down to locate the emergency shutdown button. The console tilted as he reached for it and he grimaced at the vertigo. He found the plastic cover on the button and flipped it up. His index and middle fingers hovered over the red button.

"Ready!" His voice came out muffled from the bag he was still holding to his face with his left hand.

"Lord, please don't let us come out in the middle of a star," Derek said quietly, his eyes on his watch.

"Sir?" Vicky couldn't avoid the view in her rapidly narrowing periphery while watching her console to make sure she was still holding the IPS at ninety-three percent capacity. She was starting to feel very sick.

"Eighteen . . . nineteen . . . Now!"

Jacob pressed the button and the IPS shut down. The *Pioneer* stopped accelerating and they were back to pulling zero Gs. Jacob vomited immediately, and the sound forced Vicky to reach for her own bag. She closed her eyes and took quick, shallow breaths, fighting with all her being not to throw up. She shivered, beads of sweat forming on her forehead and clumping together with no gravity to pull them down her face.

"Hey!" Derek's yell got Vicky and Jacob's attention. "We do not have time for this! We have to patch the ship!" He took a deep breath and swapped out his Command Capsule mask for one attached to a portable tank he'd stowed by his seat.

Vicky and Jacob fumbled to catch up with Derek, Jacob tying off his vomit bag and leaving it floating. They switched to their portable oxygen tanks and Jacob turned off the capsule's system. They joined Derek in a sweep of the ship, looking for the points of breach. There were seven in all; most tiny pock-marks that were patched quickly, but there was one larger pair of holes from a through-and-through breach near the airlock. Vicky and Jacob plugged the matching leaks while Derek moved back to the Command Capsule to check their systems status and power levels. Finally, the breach alarm shut off. Derek came through the access tunnel to give Vicky and Jacob an update while they reinforced their patch jobs.

Power rising, he signed, the three of them still wearing their portable oxygen masks while the ship regained its equilibrium. *Light.* He indicated a patch shining through one of the habitat windows.

Jacob finished his work and glided to the nearest right-side window, where the light was coming from. He had to look away almost immediately because of the brightness, and fumbled with the sun shade to try again.

"Umph."

Out the window, he could see a star burning reddish-orange—another red dwarf, redder than the last one. It took up far more of the view than could possibly be safe.

Jacob ripped his mask off. "We need a wider orbit!" he yelled, just as the spacecraft's internal monitoring system signaled a return to normal pressure and atmosphere levels with three loud tones.

"How much wider?" Derek asked as he and Vicky removed their own masks and shut off their tanks.

Jacob turned around and snaked back through the access tunnel, knowing the others would follow him. "A lot! We should probably use the IPS to do it."

"No," Vicky argued. "It needs time to recover from the emergency shutdown."

Jacob strapped himself in. "We have to be getting a ton of radiation."

"If the levels were imminently dangerous the system would tell us," Derek said calmly.

"The onboard system can't account for exposure duration—we need Ground Control for that. And what if the levels are only acceptable right now because we're not getting hit with the extra radiation of a flare or a gust of solar wind?"

"We can't initialize the IPS again until the battery has recharged a little," Derek said. His unruffled demeanor brought Jacob's blood pressure down a notch. "Sit tight. We'll maneuver as soon as we can, but we're not going anywhere just yet."

Silence settled over the Command Capsule. Jacob started to feel more than a little sheepish at the way he'd reacted to their proximity to the star. Vicky, he noted with chagrin, had maintained her equilibrium through it all—his was still the only vomit bag floating in the capsule and she hadn't said a word in alarm during his brief moment of panic. Jacob rolled his eyes and told himself not to worry about it.

Derek breathed deeply. That last foray through the wormhole had hit him harder than the first one, and despite his outward calm he was still feeling disoriented. He slipped an anti-nausea pill under his tongue and he pushed through the lingering vertigo to check their systems and consumables status more thoroughly. Then he forced his body to relax for a moment.

On the other side of the capsule, Vicky stared unseeing at the partial view out her window, feeling more than a little shaky. They'd had enough power to use the IPS to make another wormhole; she hadn't miscalculated. Tears

pricked her eyes, and she catalogued them as a physiological response to the stress, the nausea, and now the subse-
quent adrenaline crash. She closed her eyes and exhaled.

Jacob heard it and looked over at her. "Okay?" He said
quietly and she nodded with her eyes closed. She was fine.
She just needed a moment. They all did.

The quiet lasted all of five more seconds before Jacob
started to chuckle.

Vicky opened her eyes to look at him. "What?"

"We just . . . we just made a wormhole. On purpose! A
stable Einstein-Rosen Bridge. We decided to make one, and
we did it. And then we flew through it. Us! We flew through
an Einstein-Rosen Bridge that we created on purpose."

Vicky smiled at his boyish excitement, still too shaky
to really laugh. She took another deep breath, but she was
already feeling lighter.

"It worked," Derek agreed. "And judging by the sudden
increase in visible, white star lights, we're not in a dark nebula anymore. Good job. Both of you."

"Why, thank you, sir. Pretty sure Vic did ninety percent
of the work, though. Right?"

Vicky just stared at her console, caught by a thought.

"Hey," Jacob nudged her. "Did you hear that? Colonel
Williams just praised us and I deflected to you. You're a
rock star!"

Vicky shook her head. "We didn't get to a hundred
percent."

"Huh?"

"On the IPS. We didn't get to a hundred percent before
the wormhole formed."

Derek leaned forward against his restraints to make eye

contact with Vicky. "Ninety some-odd percent, right?"

"Ninety-three."

"That tracks, actually," Jacob mused. "We were already going faster than the first time. Maybe it didn't take us as long to compress the matter cushion because of our higher velocity."

Derek looked out his window, thoughtful. "Are we sure we were running at a hundred percent the first time before the stars changed? We didn't miss something?"

"I'm sure," Vicky said firmly. "We were definitely still experiencing normal spaceflight at the ninety percent benchmark, and we'd been running at full capacity for a minute or two before those Caution and Warnings went off."

"Always nice when the mysteries compound," Jacob said cheerfully. "But hey! We're still alive, and if we're dangerously close to a star, at least we're not dead! Yet . . ."

Derek sighed. "We'll move when the battery hits fifty percent. It won't be long."

"We should change the bubble tubes," Vicky said.

"We'll do it once we're in a wider orbit," Derek countered. "So it's not contaminated by current levels."

"Contaminated." Jacob wrinkled his nose. "Not your best choice of words, sir."

Derek ignored him. "At the rate the gauge has been rising, we should be good to go in just a couple more minutes. Abrams? Is that enough time for engine recovery?"

"I think so."

"Great. You want to run the IPS start-up checklist so we're ready?"

"Sure." Vicky got the checklist out and started running through the steps again, albeit at a more reasonable pace.

"So Mendez, what kind of star do we have?" Derek asked.

"Oh, another red dwarf. Really red. Okay if I take a spectrometer reading?"

"Be quick."

Jacob saluted crisply and Derek automatically reached up to return the gesture, catching himself just before his fingertips touched his brow. He sighed and completed the movement half-heartedly even though Jacob was already out of his seat and heading to the access tunnel. Derek checked the power gauge again and noted with satisfaction that it was still rising steadily. They'd dipped down to just eleven percent during their use of the IPS. Even with the habitat powered down to Protocol Three, they wouldn't have lasted very long if they hadn't ended up so close to a star. Close, but not inside the star. He smiled to himself at the answered prayer and silently gave thanks before allowing his mind to shift to what they'd need to do next, forming a mental list: Move to a safer orbit; EVA to repair the damaged solar array and anything else that needed to be fixed; and they'd lost more oxygen and nitrogen from the hull breaches, so eventually they would need to EVA again to scavenge the MSM.

"Ready, sir." Vicky's voice interrupted Derek's thoughts and he pushed them to the side for the time being. The needle on the power gauge was at fifty-one percent and still rising.

"Mendez! You done? It's time to go!"

Jacob's muffled reply preceded him. He came into the Command Capsule with the hand-held spectrometer still in his hands. He secured it by its Velcro strap to a bar designed for that purpose on the back of his chair and got himself strapped in.

"It's definitely a red dwarf. I didn't have much time to do any calculations," he said, "but I think we want to get at least another hundred thousand miles away. So, running the IPS at . . . ?"

"Let's keep it low," Derek supplied. "Ten percent."

"At ten percent we should cruise for about . . . let's see, how fast are we going right now?" Jacob check his navigational data and grabbed his notebook to do the math. When he was finished, he handed it to Vicky for a double-check.

"What do you think? Would running it for about fifteen seconds be enough?"

Vicky shook her head. "It would be if the engine were operating within normal parameters. With the magnets out of alignment and building up a wall of matter in front of us, we should go a little longer to be sure."

"Right. I didn't think of that. Um, how long then?"

Vicky shrugged. "Maybe twenty, twenty-five seconds? I can only guesstimate. And then a normal shutdown would probably be a good idea—the emergency cutoffs are hard on the engine and could further disturb the magnet alignment."

"Does your estimate include the shutdown time?" Derek asked.

"No."

"Alright. Let's go for twenty seconds, then, and see where we're at."

Vicky waited until Jacob was strapped in. Derek gave her a nod of approval and she pressed the final button to engage the IPS, and they were accelerating once more.

CHAPTER TWENTY-TWO

Jeff Marshall couldn't keep the grin off his face. He flipped through the pages that constituted the new communications protocol Bravo Crew and their two teams of scientists had drafted with a giddy sense of awe.

He reached the end and turned to Liz. "You've been over all this?"

"With a fine-tooth comb," she assured him. "We're confident we've come up with the best plan possible. Hopefully they'll catch on quick."

"And you're sure about these long delays between messages?"

Professor Coldwell took a step forward. "Doctor Archer requested that, Colonel Marshall. We want to give the crew ample time to decipher our messages, especially at first. This will keep the lines of communication clear."

"We'll start with radio-formatted comms," Liz said, "to maximize their ability to recognize what we're doing. We'll send the 'radio call' every half hour until they figure it out. Once they've sent the appropriate response, we'll start sending the instructions for communications."

"We'll be using Morse, correct?"

"At first," Liz said. "But we'll want to switch as quickly

as practical to something more efficient."

Jeff looked at Liz askance. "More efficient than Morse?"

"Given the parameters and restrictions of the experiment, yes. There is one existing option we're holding in reserve," she said, "but Doctor Andrews believes we can develop a better system. She and her team are still working on that."

Jeff frowned. "I'm not sure I like the idea of switching between multiple communication methods," he said. "Let's not introduce the one in reserve until we're confident there's nothing better."

"Yes, sir."

Jeff went back over the first page of the procedure. "So we start by ending the Mars program."

"That's right," Professor Coldwell said. "That should get the crew's attention."

"And then '*Pioneer*, Ground, comm check?'"

Liz nodded. "Yes. A standard radio call to establish contact, just sent over a different medium."

Jeff smiled at her. "Was that your idea?"

"James again," she corrected. "I put him on the initial contact team."

"We were all debating what kind of message to send to maximize their ability to recognize the digitized Morse," Professor Coldwell said. "Doctor Archer pointed out that the pattern recognition they have with standardized radio communications might help them decipher the message more quickly if we sent what they would expect to hear in a contact attempt."

"Excellent work." Jeff handed the stapled packet of instructions back to Liz and consulted his watch. "How much time do you need to get set up?"

"We want to send it to Charlie Crew in the simulator first," Liz said. "I asked, and they have a mock-up of the experiment with them. The simulations team wrote a program to simulate the measurements, so all we have to do is tell it what state to record and they'll see it in their log."

"This seems pretty straightforward. You want to simulate it first because . . . ?"

"We want to check our schedule for sending and receiving communications. We don't know how long it will take the crew to process our message and figure out how to send a response, but at least we can get an idea and see if our current proposed schedule is reasonable."

"Got it." Jeff checked the time on the large digital clocks at the front of the room. "Charlie Crew should still be in the simulator. Let's get this done before close of business today—I want to talk to our crew."

"We'll go right now," Liz said, and she and Dr. Coldwell left.

The professor's initial contact team was waiting in the hall. They straightened up and grew silent at the sight of the two women emerging from Ground Control.

"We're going to Simulations," Liz said. "Colonel Marshall has approved our request to test the protocol on Charlie Crew."

James gestured down the hall. "Right this way."

Liz walked with them as far as the exterior doors. "Let me know as soon as you're ready to take the experiment to Ground Control and try contacting the *Pioneer*," she told James.

"Absolutely. Are you going to check on the other team?"

"Yes."

"Tell them I said hi," he said. "In Morse binary, please."

"Ha ha."

James grinned and led the group out the doors to head to Simulations. Liz walked against the tide and headed back to the conference room where Stephanie's group was still attempting to come up with a more efficient binary system than Bacon's Cipher. When she arrived, the group was discussing how to convey mathematical symbols that might be needed to give the *Pioneer* instructions on getting home.

"Maybe math is the key," one of the computer scientists said. "Can we communicate via equations somehow? Or use a sort of number key, maybe, instead of letters?"

Paul pursed his lips in doubt. "We're going to need letters at some point," he said.

"I mean to stand in for letters," the other man said, sounding irritated.

"Two layers of decryption?" one of the linguists said, and the computer scientist abandoned his idea with a deep frown.

"Maybe we can combine Bacon's Cipher with some kind of grid system," Stephanie mused. "A five-by-five-point square for example."

She began marking up the board with different systems as a visual. Paul frowned at the squares. They wouldn't work. He could see that as Stephanie continued trying new configurations, but the basic idea of using a grid made sense somehow. Then it clicked.

"Braille!"

The group turned to look at him as one.

"Colonel Williams knows Braille," he said, unable to

articulate the thought further while his brain tried to catch up with itself.

"Oh, my..." Liz stared at him, mouth open. She couldn't believe she hadn't thought of that.

Stephanie nodded slowly. "Braille is a true binary system," she acknowledged, "but it's a six-point grid. That's not as efficient as Bacon's Cipher."

"But Braille is chock-full of abbreviations," Liz said. "We can shorten words, prefixes, suffixes—it's all standardized and Colonel Williams is proficient. It's perfect! Braille can express punctuation, mathematical symbols—even emphasis. It does everything we need! All the groundwork is laid out for us—we just have to figure out how to translate the dots to ones and zeroes."

"And get a list of those abbreviations," Paul added, his face all lit up with excitement.

"That's what the internet is for," Liz said, bouncing on her heels. She turned to the computer scientists. "Can you write a program that will allow us to type a phrase and have the computer automatically apply the standardized abbreviations?"

"Chuck can, once we know what the abbreviations are," said the linguist who'd backed Paul up about communicating with only numbers, gesturing towards one of her colleagues. "He's a computational linguist, does this sort of thing in his sleep!"

Liz turned to Stephanie. "What do you think?"

The linguist was smiling now. "I think this could really work. It uses a system already familiar to a member of the crew and with the abbreviations, it should be pretty efficient."

"The question is how to express the dots in binary," Paul said.

"Actually, that's easy." Stephanie drew two columns of three dots on the white board. "The dots are read left to right, top to bottom. So the upper left dot is 'one,' the middle left dot is 'two,' the bottom left dot is 'three,' and then you go back up to the top. The top right dot is 'four,' and so on."

"But we only have ones and zeroes to work with," one of the other linguists objected. "Not one, two, and threes."

"Yes, but we don't need to use the actual numbers. We only need the directionality. Look. If we call a raised dot a one and the not-raised dots zeroes, we just write them in the cell order. Like this."

She drew a new six-point grid, but this time she drew empty circles instead of dots, then colored in the top two circles and the middle right circle.

"That's the letter 'd,'" she said. "We can express it like this: one, zero, zero, one, one, zero."

"That's perfect," Liz said, amazed at how easy it was. "All we have to do is tell them in Morse that we're going to switch to Braille and give an example, like this. One letter should be enough."

Stephanie spread her arms out to encompass the whole group, like a minister giving the blessing at the end of a church service. "I need whatever the Braille equivalent is to a dictionary, and I need a MATLAB script or plugin with all the letters, numbers, symbols, abbreviations—everything. It all needs to be transcribed into this binary system," she finished, pointing at the 1s and 0s she'd written to spell out the letter "d."

As the programmers and linguists got to work in a flurry of activity, Liz moved to stand beside Paul.

"Nicely done, Major."

Paul shrugged off the praise. "This only works because of Colonel Williams' knowledge of Braille," he pointed out. "I'm just glad we can do it!"

"I'm glad you thought of it at all."

"Yeah." Paul watched as Stephanie's team started analyzing charts of the Braille alphabet on their computer screens and writing scripts for MATLAB. "Doctor Andrews was drawing the squares and it just sort of popped into my head," he said. He turned to face her head-on, his eyes bright with anticipation. "We're going to talk to the crew," he said.

Liz returned his smile without reservation, reaching out to briefly squeeze his arm. They were finally going to be back in communication with the *Pioneer*, and they were symbolically breaking the laws of physics and quantum mechanics to do it. She took a deep breath and came back to herself.

"I better go let Jeff know."

On the *Pioneer*, all was quiet. Once they'd settled into what they estimated to be a comfortable orbit around their new red dwarf star and set up the bubble test tubes to verify their safety, Derek had allowed Vicky to power the habitat back up to full capacity. Their battery levels had started dropping again, but very slowly; shutting down a few nonessential systems like the main lights had solved the problem. Once again, none of them had slept in a while, so Derek ordered rest for everyone. And since they were no longer flying through frequent barrages of debris, they could truly relax.

Derek grabbed a snack from the kitchen and situated himself at the small table with Jacob, who was typing rapidly on his laptop when Vicky emerged from the bathroom in her workout clothes. She watched him for a moment, curious.

"What are you typing?"

Jacob finished the sentence he was writing and looked up. "My journal."

"You keep a journal? Since when?"

"I started it a couple days after we left the solar system. Everything was super hectic at first, but once we settled in for the long haul, I guess the significance of it sunk in and I thought there should be some sort of historical record of our . . . adventure, for lack of a better word. But I haven't had time to write anything since the Dust Cloud of Death damaged the solar panels." He shrugged. "It's not exactly a 'Captain's log,' but it'll do."

Vicky narrowed her eyes at him. "Was that a *Star Trek* reference?"

"Yeah. I'm impressed you got it," Jacob said, his voice reflecting his surprise. "You watch?"

"My brother and I watched *Next Generation* when we were kids," she said. "I haven't seen it in . . . wow. More than two decades."

"Who was your favorite character?"

"Data."

"Really." Jacob crossed his arms. "I would've thought you'd like Geordi La Forge best. He was an engineer."

"Data was an android," Vicky argued. "You can't get cooler than that."

Jacob chuckled. "You ever see *Dark Matter*?"

"No. Why?"

"There's an android. She was my favorite character on that show."

"See? You can't top the androids."

"I guess not. What about you, sir?"

"*Almost Human*," Derek said with a straight face.

"What?"

"It's a movie about a humanoid robot who decides to leave the nest and go to college."

Vicky stifled a laugh as Jacob sputtered.

"No, I . . . I didn't . . . I meant *Star Trek*. Did you ever watch?"

Derek shrugged. "I'm more of a *Star Wars* fan, but I've seen my fair share of *Trek*—my son was really into it when he was a kid." He crumpled up his trash to get the air out before throwing it away. "My favorite character from *Next Gen* was Worf. I loved all the cultural conflicts that happened with a Klingon aboard."

"Yeah, he was pretty cool."

The crew fell silent and a subtle tension crept into the module, as if their light-hearted conversation had been the only thing keeping it at bay.

"Well, I'll let you get back to your journal," Vicky said lamely and went to their tiny gym, trying to block out the suddenly bittersweet memories of watching science fiction with her brother. She was unfolding the treadmill from the wall of the habitat when the EPE computer beeped. Everyone froze for a second and just looked at each other. Derek recovered first and reached out to snag the experiment by the Velcro strap holding it more or less in place over the tiny refrigerator next to the table. He turned on the screen and frowned at the pop-up notification from MarsLab, telling him that Earth had sent the program termination code.

"That's odd," he said.

"What is?" Jacob leaned over to see. "Program termination code? Why would they terminate the program?"

Vicky abandoned the treadmill. "You don't think it's an error, do you?"

"Did the particles get disentangled?"

"Just relax," Derek said, swallowing his own worry for their sakes. "The particles did not disentangle and there's no error—this is a preprogrammed sequence that they just chose to execute for some reason. Let's not read too much into it."

The measurement program log began to populate with 0s as well as the standard 1s, and Derek had to eat his words.

"Alright, something's going on here. Jacob, can you transcribe this?"

"Sure." Jacob typed the sequence of numbers into his journal as the most expedient method of copying them down. When they hit ten 1s in a row, Derek told him to stop; they'd gone back to the status quo.

"What do you have?" he asked.

Jacob turned the computer so he could see.

There was a very long sequence of alternating 1s and 0s. It started out looking like a pattern: three 1s followed by three 0s, then another set of three 1s and 0s. After that the sequence seemed random, but it ended the same way it had started.

"What are they doing?" Jacob asked, completely baffled. "Is there another preset program we don't know about?"

"There could be," Derek said, "but nothing's popping up. If it's a pre-set program and that's the correct activation code, I think it would have triggered the program to run."

Jacob scrunched up his face in concentration. "Maybe they're trying to talk to us."

Vicky frowned. "Bit of a leap."

Jacob acknowledged her point with a head tilt and Derek noted the cordiality of their minor clash with satisfaction. When he looked back at the screen, the sequence had started again. They tracked along with it to verify it was the same as the first time, and that erased any suspicion that it might be random.

"Okay," Vicky said. "Let's think this through. If they are trying to communicate with us, how would they go about it?"

"It would have to be a binary system," Jacob said.

Derek snapped his fingers. "Morse code," he said, triumphant. "It's simple, we all know it—it has to be Morse."

Vicky moved to crowd around the laptop with Jacob and Derek. They talked through the sequence, deciding that a single 1 followed by a 0 must represent a dot while the triple 1s and 0s represented dashes. Jacob transcribed the sequence accordingly, his heart fairly pounding with the excitement of it.

"Okay, here's what we've got: PNRG RDCC. What on earth does that mean?"

"It has to be something we'd understand," Vicky reasoned. She felt like the solution was right there in front of her, but she couldn't for the life of her figure it out. Beside her, Jacob mouthed the letters over and over again.

It was Derek who figured it out. "It's a radio call! PNR GRD CC—*Pioneer*, Ground, comm check. It's a standard comm check!"

Vicky and Jacob stared at him, stunned.

"What do we say?" Vicky asked almost frantically.

"We respond like we would to voice comms: Ground, *Pioneer*, five by five. But we'll abbreviate it like they did. Here."

Derek took Jacob's laptop and typed out GRD PNR 5X5. He converted it to dashes and dots, then he started typing it out in binary.

"This better go a lot quicker once we get some practice," he grumbled.

"Maybe we can write a plugin for MATLAB to convert it for us," Vicky murmured.

When Derek had finished, he paused, realizing he didn't know how to manually tell the experiment computer when to take measurements of the particles to change their state.

"Abrams, is there a manual override to this thing?"

"Yes! Hold on!" Vicky zoomed away to get her laptop and pulled up her notes on the EPE. "Okay, go to the EPE's main program. In the settings menu, you should be able to toggle to manual. It'll ask for a verification code."

"Do you have it?" Derek asked, finding the menu.

"Yes."

"What is it?"

Vicky read the code and Derek typed it in successfully. The program opened a new window with a button Derek could press to tell it to take a measurement.

"Crap, when was the last measurement?" he asked, frantically pulling up the log. He checked the timestamp of the last entry and toggled back to the EPE program, noting with intense relief that there was digital clock with a seconds counter in the GUI. He'd need to make the next measurement in two seconds to start the sequence without flooding the Alice computer with false state changes.

Vicky and Jacob kept quiet, tracking his actions but not breaking his concentration.

"There," he said when he finally finished sending the sequence and put the measurement program back on automatic, exhausted from the concentration it had required. "Reply sent. Now we just wait for the next message."

"How long do you think?" Jacob asked, chewing on his lip.

"Probably a while," Derek said, calming down. "They'll probably have already worked out a schedule and they'll stick to it, just to make sure we don't get our proverbial wires crossed."

"And they'll have plenty of lag time worked into that schedule," Jacob concluded. "So it'll be a while."

"Exactly. I'd guess at least half an hour."

Vicky shook her head, still dazed. "They figured out how to talk to us," she said. "I can't believe we didn't think of this."

"Oh, I wouldn't feel too bad," Derek said dryly.

"Yeah! We broke the ice with the Mars program, after all," Jacob pointed out. "Besides, we were a little too busy plugging leaks to dream up an idea like this. And creating wormholes! On purpose."

That brought a smile to Vicky's face, even as she rolled her eyes.

Derek chucked. He folded his arms across his chest and looked at his crewmates. "We're not alone in this anymore," he said. "We've reestablished communications with Ground Control now—all because we took initiative to retrieve the EPE. We set that in motion, together. And because of that, we're not alone anymore."

Vicky blinked back sudden tears and Jacob found the effect contagious. He clapped his hands together to lighten the mood.

"Well," he said loudly, "this is officially the best day of my life. Can I just say, I love you guys. You are amazing, and I love you both."

Vicky laughed and sniffed, and Derek decided a little celebration might do them all good.

"Mendez," he said in his best official command voice.

"Sir?"

"I think this calls for chocolate pudding, don't you?"

Jacob grinned even wider. "Yes, sir!"

Derek set the EPE aside, carefully anchoring it in place nearby, and Vicky got settled at the table next to him. Jacob joined them, bearing three chocolate pudding pouches.

"Monsieur. Mademoiselle." He handed each of them a pouch with a flourish.

"Merci," Vicky said, amused by the mock ceremony of the presentation.

Jacob removed the tab from the top of his pudding pouch. "Sir?" he said. "Would you like to give a toast?"

"I would," Derek said, playing along. He cleared his throat conspicuously and raised his own opened pouch.

The others copied his gesture. "To the entangled particles experiment. We take back everything we ever said about you. To the EPE!"

"To the EPE!" Vicky and Jacob echoed, "clinking" pouches with Derek. Vicky shook her head at his uncharacteristic silliness as she removed her pouch's tab and sucked some of the pudding out, but as she looked around the table at her happy teammates, Jacob pretending to faint with pleasure as he ate his pudding, Vicky told herself to just enjoy the moment. She focused on Derek's carefree smile and Jacob's ridiculous antics. They all forgot for a moment that they were still unknown lightyears from home as they proposed and made toasts to the Mars Service Module, MIT, Ground Control, and even the red dwarf star they were orbiting, which Jacob spontaneously dubbed Bombur.

"To Bombur!" they chorused, "clinking" pouches again. For the next few minutes, the spacecraft vibrated with laughter. It didn't matter that they were orbiting a foreign star, or that there was no guarantee the Hawking Engine would ever bring them home. All that mattered was the fact that they were no longer completely cut off from Earth. They were together, they were in a relatively stable position, and they could finally talk to Ground Control again. As they drifted into the unknown, their hopes ran high, and for the moment, that was all they needed.

ACKNOWLEDGMENTS

My first thanks must go to my parents, Ron and Penny, without whose support I would not have been able to write this novel. My second thanks goes to my brother Steven, who gave so generously of his time to act as my science adviser. While all purposeful fictionalizations and accidental mistakes alike are my own, everything right about the science in this book is thanks to him. I also want to thank my brother Ben and my sisters-in-law, Meredith and Saisai, for always being so supportive.

Many thanks to my editor, Ryan Boyd, for his comments, suggestions and encouragement, and to my beta readers—principally Adam McCoy, for his enthusiasm and detailed feedback. Finally, I would like to thank the incredibly talented Christopher Doll, Hillary Manton Lodge, Kyle Shepherd, and Leigh Thomas. Your hard work took this project to the next level.

ABOUT THE AUTHOR

Rachel Lulich is a writer, freelance editor, and Air Force veteran. She has a Master's Degree in Book Publishing and has written for *Clarinet News* magazine, *Short and Sweet: A Different Beat*, and Gateworld.net, and has edited several award-winning books. *Random Walk* is her debut novel.

CPSIA information can be obtained
at www.ICGtesting.com
Printed in the USA
FSHW012257121219
65037FS